For Olivia

All The Best

14/06/2022, London

Dr. [illegible]

DEADLINE

ERKUT SOGUT

CA PUBLISHING

This is a work of fiction. Names, characters, places, and incidents either are the product of the author's imagination or are used fictitiously. Any resemblance to actual persons, living or dead, events, or locales is entirely coincidental.

First published in Great Britain in 2022, by CA Publishing House Ltd

Typesetting by Tom Witcomb
Cover Design by Nick Castle

ISBN 978-1-7397288-0-9

CA Publishing House
Summit House,170 Finchley Road
London, United Kingdom
NW3 6BP

www.erkutsogut.com

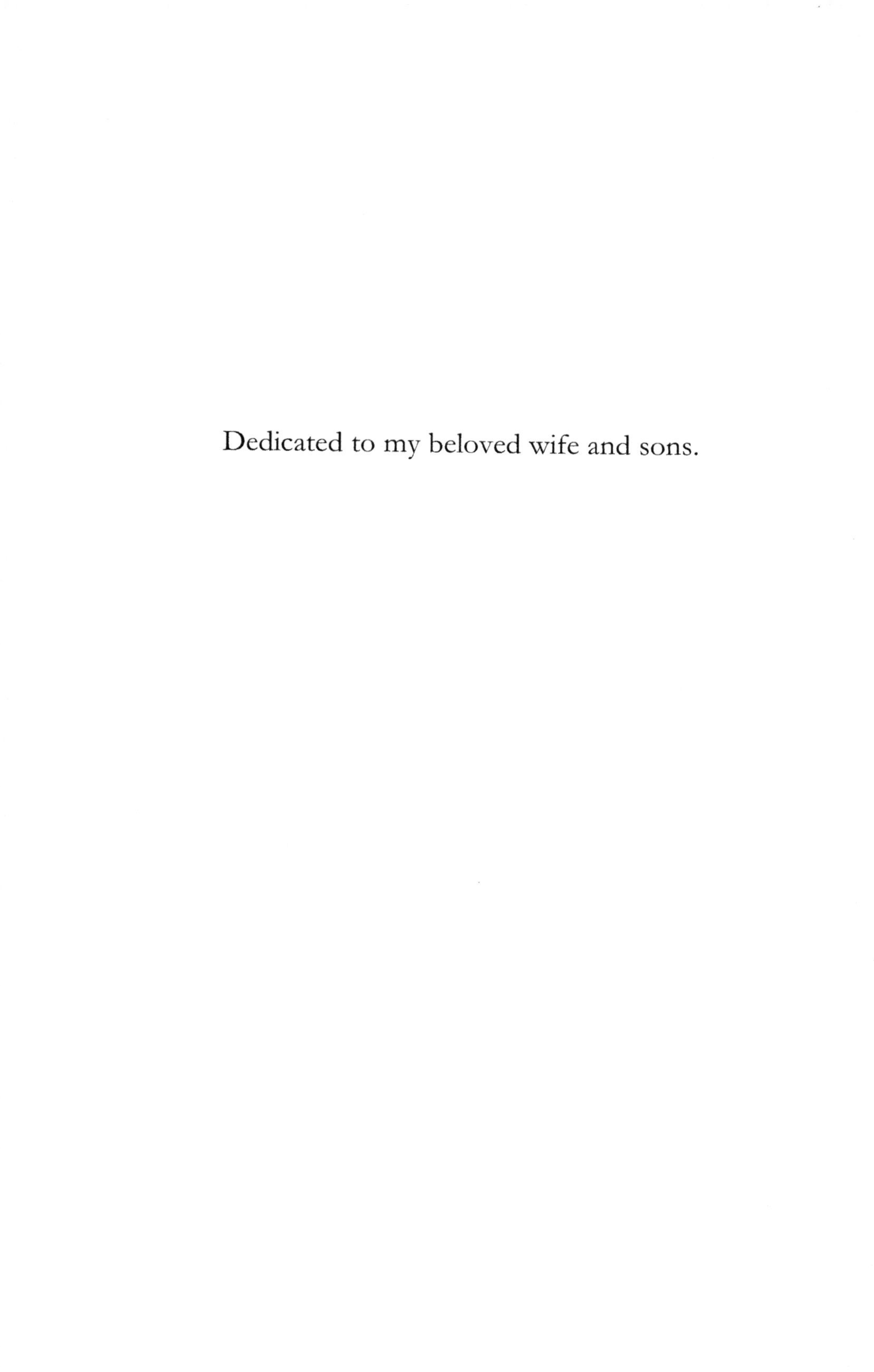

Dedicated to my beloved wife and sons.

I

Ander Anaia watched out through a wall of glass as the sun rose over La Concha Bay. He sipped quietly on his coffee, preparing himself for the next forty-eight hours. He breathed in and closed his eyes, allowing himself to calm. He could do this. Just a few more days and he'd be at The Table. A few more days and he'd be granted unimaginable power. All doors would be open to him.

The noise of the espresso machine kicked in from the kitchen behind him and jolted him out of his revery. Joska stood there – the makeup around her eyes was still smeared.

The ceramic burrs chewed at the coffee beans, kicking the fine dust into the portafilter. She gently tamped the coffee down and locked it into the La Marzocco machine that sat in pride of place on the countertop. Placing a glistening white tulip cup beneath the filter, she set the machine in motion.

The rich aroma of almonds and chocolate filled the air as the black-brown liquid filled her cup. She picked it up, brought it to her nose and took a sip before walking over to Ander.

"Morning, dad." She followed his gaze across the bay.

"My love, how are you feeling? Did you sleep?" Ander placed his arm around his daughter. "I see you found something to wear…" he laughed as he noticed his daughter's reflection. She didn't stay with him often, but he had kept a room for her exactly the same as she had left it. That had been years ago. The wardrobe hadn't been touched either, so was filled with the sartorial whims of a fourteen-year old girl. In this case a pair of shorts that barely fit her and a t-shirt that would have once been baggy but now fit a little too snug.

"Eventually. The coffee will help. When do you have to leave?"

"Soon. There are fresh towels, food in the cupboards. You can stay as long as you like. You know that."

She grabbed his arm and squeezed it around her tightly for a moment, remembering how safe he had always made her feel as a child. A car horn sounded outside, breaking the moment.

"Say hi to Uncle Marco, *aita*."

"I'll be back tomorrow, *maitea*. Enjoy the beach." Ander wheeled his case across the expansive parquet floor, opening the double-width front door and breathing in the fresh air. He was ready.

Joska walked back through to the kitchen placed her espresso cup on the side. She checked her phone, ignoring the several missed calls from her mother and placed it back into her bra.

She moved back to the bedroom to get changed, walking through to the en suite and turning on the shower. As she began to undress, she walked over to her old CD player and switched it on smiling as she picked up the beat of the music and started sashaying around the room, embracing the opportunity to be a kid again. When things were more innocent.

Remembering the towels, Joska went out to the long corridor that connected the open plan kitchen lounge to the bedrooms and opened the airing cupboard. She felt a breeze on her skin, and it took her a second to realise that her father hadn't closed the door properly. She walked down the hall, her bare feet cold on the parquet and closed it again, double locking the latch, and picked up her towel as she made her way back to her room.

Steam was trickling beneath the bathroom door, which Joska opened to a backdraft of vapour. She moved over to the sink and opened the mirrored bathroom cabinet, taking out cotton wool and some make-up remover. One hand wiped the condensation that had formed on the mirror, the other wiped a cotton pad across her eyes, the cooling cucumber micellar water washing away the evidence of last night's emotional conversations.

She didn't know why her mother had to be the way she was. Why she seemed to want to stand in her way on every last thing. If Joska wanted to study to be a veterinarian then why couldn't she? It was a world away from her mother's glamorous brunches and sponsored social media posts. It was a better life, more fulfilling. She had never enjoyed the excesses that her father's wealth had afforded their family. Even now they were divorced, her mum managed to afford a lavish lifestyle. God knows why her dad still founded it.

She closed her eyes and rubbed the cotton wool over them again.

So she didn't see the dark figure move behind her, obscured in the condensation that had reformed on the mirror's surface.

A hand reached around her mouth and muffled her scream. A sharp prick and she felt her head go light, her eyelids drooping. She mustered the ounce of strength she'd been left with and pushed back against her attacker, and they slipped on the wet tiled floor.

Joska landed hard on his chest, but he held on fast. Moments later, she felt her whole body relax and the world around went dark.

2

David Miller sat and watched through his office window as three pigeons pecked their way around the green square of lawn in Hanover Square, picking up remnants of the lunches the workers in the office buildings around the square had absent-mindedly eaten as they flicked through social media and news updates on their cell phones.

He snapped out of his pigeon-gaze; he did not have time for daydreaming. He had received an offer from Manchester United. He had reread the terms and reread them again. He made a list for himself of everything that still needed to be sorted and finalised.

It was early afternoon already and tomorrow, at 6pm, the summer transfer window would close in England. He had to be quick and precise with his decisions.

Almost everything was prepared and the one-way business class ticket from Dusseldorf to Manchester for Patrick had been arranged by the club officials last night. He was due to land later this afternoon in Manchester. David would take the train so that they could meet at the hotel after his arrival. On the face of it, nothing could stop this deal anymore, yet David had a strange feeling about it.

He had been in the office early. He was a man of routine, something bred into him by his German mother and her tendency for discipline and order. One of many traditions she was proud to impart on her son. Ones that he felt he owed it to her memory to uphold.

Every morning he would roll out of bed and spend the next hour reading anything from the news to books, to history, to languages, law or economics. He would then push himself on a five mile run before showering and eating a hearty breakfast.

He was often alone in the office for a while, waiting for his two colleagues to join him once they'd eventually got out of bed.

The three had met at Oxford University as they studied for their master's in international law. That was three years ago now and after exploring different routes they had each decided to start their own businesses and had moved to London together. By sharing an office – and an apartment – they had been able to save money and help each other on their journeys.

David stared at the clock. Anxiety was creeping in. This was set to be a deal that would break him out as a rising star in his world. It had to come off. But not just for him, for Patrick as well. Patrick had been his first ever client, when David made the decision to be a football agent. He had discovered him on a trip to Germany to see his mother's family. He had stopped off at a local football club and been astounded by the talent Patrick showed. He dominated the game, following the forwards with a dogged determination and putting in precise crunching tackles that won back the ball and told the wingers to think again before they tried to lose him. David had walked into the changing rooms after the game and introduced himself and the two had instantly hit it off. It didn't take long for news to spread about Patrick, and soon he was playing top-tier football in Germany.

United's officials had assured David that all the necessary details were in place and that the required contracts would be signed on the last day of the transfer window.

David questioned the need to leave it until the last minute, and his mind raced with all the things that might go wrong between now and six o'clock tomorrow.

The only explanation he'd been given was that the large volume of ongoing transfers at the moment had caused the delay. He wasn't really convinced but he had to believe it. He had no other choice. The next day and a half would unfold in front of him, he would control what he could and do his very best to get his deal done.

***

"Couldn't we have done that later? We have the entire day ahead of us," said Jose, wearily rubbing his bloodshot eyes as he steadily worked through documents that David had given him to double check.

David watched him, exasperated. "Jose, it's almost 2pm! Please tell me you didn't go out last night? Every minute is important today!" He made every effort to clearly emphasise the magnitude of the day ahead.

Jose looked up at him sheepishly, "Si, Amigo – you know every Wednesday is Latino Night. I couldn't miss that. But I made sure I was back by 4am."

"You can have a siesta later this afternoon when I leave for Manchester," said David with a shake of the head and a wry smile.

"Si, si, claro amigo."

David turned to William. "What about you, mate? Are you ok?" William looked pale and unwell; his eyes a similar bloodshot to Jose's.

"I'm all good, Davey-boy," he responded with an exaggerated effort to sound buoyant. David still sometimes had difficulties understanding William – a young sports lawyer originally from Glasgow — especially when he spoke too fast, but the two had become firm friends. It was hard not to like him; William was always one for a joke and was always a pleasure to have around.

"Don't worry about me. Just had a couple of drinks in the pub before bed."

He looked down, trying to appear busy and avoid further questioning.

"What happened to not drinking in the week?" David laughed.

William looked awkward, "Only if there's a special occasion, David."

"And what was so special about last night?" David asked with a smirk. There had been a few 'special nights' recently.

"Ah, well..." William spluttered as he sipped on his coffee, "The landlord, Sam, I think you might know him? It was his wife's birthday, and I was invited too. I had to go and have some drinks to be polite, right?"

David sighed before breaking into a friendlier smile.

He firmly grasped William's shoulder, "Please, just check the final documents one more time. Then we can go through them together. I have to make a quick call."

"Your mysterious journalist friend?" asked William smiling, pushing his luck and trying to lighten the conversation.

"Yes, don't even try. She'll introduce herself to you guys when the time is right. I promised her I wouldn't tell you anything until then."

David left the office and walked past the Statue of Pitt the Younger. His mind wandered. Pitt was just 24 years old when he was elected to lead the country. He found the story inspiring. Too often, people were told they had to wait their turn. But that was just a way of maintaining the status quo. You didn't need to. You could just take it.

David had recently taken a particular liking to a small wooden bench tucked away in the far-left corner of the square. It offered views over the entire park, and he could see his office window in the distance, but it was overarched by a large tree, providing a sufficient level of privacy.

He sat down, reached into his pocket for his mobile, took a deep breath and made the call.

The line connected after a couple of rings, "David, how are you? Is everything going well down there?"

"All good, Annabel, thanks" He usually liked talking to Annabel, catching her up on what he'd been up to. David started to get the same feeling he'd been getting recently every time he'd spoken to her. At some point he needed to tell her. It was hard to describe the feeling he had when he thought about her, but it was warm and pleasant.

But today there was little time for small talk.

"Are the contracts okay so far?" Annabel said.

"For the most part, but some of it's missing. I'm praying that they'll send everything today so we can check it's all in order. Jose and William are in the office so they are able to help out which should make the workload more manageable."

Annabel could sense David's anxiety through the phone and tried to calm him, "I'll call my guys inside the club – they might be able to help us." It was kind of her, thought David, but unless they were willing to read over contracts, he didn't know what help it could be.

Annabel saw the good in everyone. She was originally from North London; born into a liberal British-Jewish family and spent most of her life in and around Finchley. There was a large population of British-Jews in the area and from an early age she was exposed to the traditional principles and behaviours of Judaism.

Although her close family was not particularly strict with religion, she spent most weekends at the Sternberg Centre in East Finchley where she had learned Hebrew. She had encouraged her family and friends to have a Shabbat ceremony every Friday, the highlight being the delicious Challah bread that her mum made.

As she got older, despite her best efforts, the visits to the Synagogue became increasingly infrequent. Nevertheless, she stood by her Jewish beliefs and principles and planned to bring her children up under the same lifestyle one day.

This would be difficult in the Wilmslow community where she now lived. The Jewish population was scarce and there had only ever been one formal congregation recorded, right after the second World War, presumably held by evacuees.

The nearest Synagogue was in Manchester, but other than the most important Jewish celebrations she struggled to find the time to visit.

These days, she focussed all of her energy and her morals on combatting the unethical side of football, hoping to make the game a better place.

"Thanks Annabel, have you heard anything about Ander Anaia?" asked David.

"Nothing yet, but you can be sure that he's either on his way to Manchester now or already there. He wasn't listed on the manifests of any commercial flights, so he must have hired a private jet."

The stress in David's voice resurfaced, "He stopped calling me a week ago. I told you before, to begin with he was nice, and we spoke about doing deals together in the future. But now he's completely ghosted me."

"Don't worry about Anaia, David. He's not a good guy. Other than the guys from The Table, no one really likes him." She paused, considering her next words. "I've actually heard rumours that even some guys at the Table have started disliking him and the way he conducts his business. But nothing can change how influential his brother is and will continue to be."

David knew this was true, but it didn't stop him hating the fact that an unscrupulous agent could be successful just because of his famous brother.

"He was pretty aggressive last time we spoke, actually. Told me to call him in future before offering any of my players to United if I ever wanted to successfully complete a deal there."

Ander had suggested David send Patrick to La Liga and tried to pretend he was helping them. David had batted off the offer. His unwillingness to cooperate had clearly frustrated Ander who, in their last call, eventually cracked and revealed his motivation behind discouraging David.

"David," Ander had said, "You must understand that without my brother's permission, no player will be bought by or sold from the club. My brother is not just my brother, he's my client too. I negotiated his contract three years ago. I ensured that no one in the club would be able to do anything significant without his approval." David could picture Ander's smug grin on the other end of the line.

"I would suggest that it is sensible to forewarn your player that United are not interested and that you begin exploring other options before it's too late. It would also be best to let United know that they're no longer an option for your player. Do you understand?"

It only served to make David even more determined.

"I never agreed to anything he said." David assured Annabel. "I don't understand how an agent can have so much influence in a club that has a sporting director and a full management team. How could club officials ever allow that?"

"Welcome to the dark side of football," Annabel responded. She had worked this beat for years, knew the ins and outs completely. Had learned to cope with the aggressive men who thought there was no place in 'their game' for women like her.

"There are two options. Either you run away and never work as an agent again, or you fight through, establish yourself and learn how to survive. For all its benefits and brilliance, it is still a world rife with corruption, money laundering, criminals, mafia, gangs and other dirty business."

David hesitated as he briefly contemplated the options, "You have known me for long enough Annabel… What do you think I'll do?"

David heard Annabel laugh. A soft chuckle, full of warmth, some admiration, perhaps. "Well, I know you would never run away."

She was right and David knew it. He knew this was what he wanted to do and knew he was good enough to do it. He'd fight through.

"I'll see you in Manchester, Annabel." He felt buoyed by their conversation. Annabel's confidence in him had steeled his determination.

"Can't wait. To see you, of course, but also... well, you never quite know who might be listening on the phone."

"What do you mean?" David's new-found confidence was dented.

"I'll tell you later. Can't talk now. And David? Be careful."

But she had already hung up.

A sense of dread manifested in the pit of David's stomach. He slowly put his phone back into his pocket and looked took in his surroundings. A few people having a late lunch still lingered, making the most of their hour break by taking in some sunshine.

He noticed two men, dressed all in black with sunglasses helping to obscure their faces, sitting on the other side of the park.

As he caught their eye, it seemed to David that they stopped talking to one another. David turned away from them quickly, got up from his bench and began to walk back towards his office. Something about the men, about the way they looked at him had unsettled him. He cast a look back over his shoulder.

The men had got up from their seat and were making their way over to him with a determined stride.

He pulled his phone out of his pocket again, hoping it might help him. Perhaps he could call the police. His mind raced through various irrational scenarios as he computed how he would deal with each one. David broke into a trot as the two men were catching up.

As he neared the exit of the park a voice called after him, "Excuse me, sir? Just a minute."

David pretended to be preoccupied by his phone and crossed the street, barely checking for oncoming cars. A bus screamed by, missing him by a fraction, blaring its horn. Never once considering slowing down.

He reached the front of his office building and fumbled for his key card. Eventually he managed to swipe it in front of the reader. The doors seemed to take an age to open but eventually slid open. David finally walked into the entrance and breathed a sigh of relief.

He hadn't looked back again and had no idea where the men might be. He jogged up the stairs, not wanting to take the elevator in case the men made it inside and he was trapped in there with him. Inside the office he walked over to the window as beads of sweat broke over his brow. He could see no one. Just nerves. They were probably just some random guys, nothing to do with him. Why did they call out to me, then?

"What's going on, amigo?" asked Jose as David strode back into the office and began pacing up and down on the carpet.

"Nothing Jose, nothing," he replied, determined not to let his fear show as he continued to scan outside the window. "Let's just get this done, eh? Sooner the better."

The taller man made a call.

"We just saw him in the park. He was sat chatting on the phone with someone before going back into his office. We tried talking to him, but he ran away."

"Interesting, be careful. He will be leaving for Manchester soon, make sure you are there when he does."

"We are following the plan as agreed. Don't worry." The man hung up the call and immediately removed the rear of the phone case. He pried out the battery and released the SIM card, which he snapped in half and deposited in a nearby bin.

He turned to the second man and nodded down the street. The two set off through Mayfair on towards phase two of their plan.

3

Ander was still bleeding from his nose as the private jet descended into Manchester. He was used to it. Since childhood he had experienced nose bleeds, often induced and worsened by stress. They had started when he watched his dad walk into prison, leaving him behind.

Stay calm, he thought.

He took long, deep breaths and closed his eyes. The short flight felt had felt endless for him. He usually loved flying and dreamed of buying his own jet one day, perhaps when he joined The Table.

Today was an important day. The day that would ensure no one could overlook him any longer. This would be the deal of a lifetime.

As the plane landed and began to taxi, he got up from his seat and put on his jacket. The fabric embraced him as he pulled it over his shoulders, the lining flashed in the cabin light. He felt as though he were a knight pulling on armour before a battle.

The bleeding from his nose bothered him less than usual. He needed to be in Manchester as soon as possible. He had to see his brother. Time was scarce and he needed to see him face to face. He didn't want anything being traced.

"How are you, sir?" the private hostess interrupted his train of thought. "Do you need more tissues?"

Ander shook his head, "No, thanks. I'm fine now. I think its stopping," he responded, his tone polite but firm. He didn't want any more fuss over the issue.

"You are welcome, sir. We hope you enjoy your stay here."

"Thanks a lot, Gracias."

Ander made his way down the steps at the side of the plane. He was one step closer to seeing Marco.

4

"Why don't you take a private jet, David?" asked Jose, smiling, "After all, you're about to become very rich and you'll have a lot of money to spend."

Jose and William were sat huddled over their laptops whilst David packed his bag, checking and rechecking he had everything he might need over the next few days.

"Don't get too excited," David responded, a little abrupt perhaps, although he couldn't but help break into a small smile. "Nothing is finalised yet. Let's just stay focused and we might just bring this deal home."

William piped up, "Don't forget the holiday you promised us if the deal goes through. A week of luxury in Dubai, and it's all on you."

"I'll keep my word, don't worry. This is why I'm a good agent," he winked at William, "Whatever I've promised, I will follow through. You guys should know me by now."

As the others laughed and David faced the current reality again, he considered the bigger issues in life. His family was deep in debt. After his mum had died his father had gone back to Sunderland and started a small car dealership. He had borrowed from the bank and managed to persuade friends to lend him money to start the new business.

His aim had been to use his contacts in Germany to speak with some car dealers and sort some generous trades for high performance German cars. He dreamed big, but the reality was vastly different.

The bank loan had now nearly doubled with interest, and his friends were growing tired of continually asking for their money back and were gradually becoming less friendly.

His father had used the family home – where he lived with David's grandmother – as collateral against the loan for the dealership. If they couldn't pay the bank loan back soon then the house would go to the bank.

When this deal went through, David could finally help his father repay the money he owed and help him live a more stable life. The sooner the better; his dad had answered the door to several unknown people recently, demanding money off of him. Things were getting out of control.

David felt a huge amount of pressure. He needed to succeed and get this deal done. His family were relying on him. There was no other way.

"You have plenty of time, mate. Why do you want to leave so early?" William interrupted David's thoughts.

"I still need to make some phone calls. I'll keep you posted on any updates and will send you the schedule two and the dual representation agreement as soon as I have it. Stay in the office today as long as you can, please. There's plenty to do, so settle in for a long day," answered David, with a distinct look of determination.

Jose looked enthused, "We'll be following it on TV. There could be something interesting we need to know from there."

"Take care guys, we can do this," David said, turning towards the door, "I'll hopefully see you by tomorrow evening at the latest, after everything is signed and finished, we can celebrate. Thanks again for all your help."

He opened the door and left the office. He had a strange feeling bubbling in his stomach, nervousness or excitement, he wasn't sure which.

David had lied about needing to make some phone calls, he only had one he needed to make.

He tried to call his dad, but there was no answer. He tried the landline, but no one picked that up either. Nor his dad's office. He wondered where his dad and grandma would be, they didn't often leave the house. It could only be a small number of things. He assumed that his dad must have gone out for a walk with her, or to one of her weekly doctor's appointment.

David trotted down the stairs and entered the tube station. He walked through the turnstile and walked down the escalator on the left-hand side, joining the flow of travellers. The underground system had always impressed him. Sure, there was the odd delay at the end of a long day, but generally, things ran like clockwork as people flowed through the warren of interlocking tunnels that served the city.

He was on autopilot as he moved through the station, onto the platform, onto the train, and before he knew it, he was emerging onto the grand concourse at Euston station.

Inside the grand hall he looked up at the huge display screens that showed departure times in bright yellow typography. There was still no platform information for his train to Manchester.

"Typical," David muttered to himself.

His fellow passengers stood around patiently waiting for the information, and as each platform came up the crowd would thin as people rushed off to make sure they caught their train and got a seat.

Stupid system, he thought as he looked around at the rest of the station for a place to get coffee.

David tried to avoid chain coffee places at all costs. He loved local, small independents run by people that really understood what they were serving.

Coffee-making was a fine art and David was a self-acclaimed critic. The making process was important, it impacted the coffee, and he could taste it if it wasn't done with the care it deserved. You didn't get that at a chain.

He had spent lots of his time in London exercising his coffee-connoisseur skills in countless different coffee boutiques and had narrowed it down to one favourite spot. 39 Steps Coffee in Knightsbridge, just opposite Harrods. It was the ideal spot to have a great coffee and to meet people during the working day, but coffee was not the only reason he went there frequently. It had a reputation of being a popular hangout for agents, coaches, players and club officials in London.

David found a bench with a view of the display screens, took a seat and tried to clear his mind of the earlier incident, but couldn't quite shake it. Who were those men? He was certain they were calling out to him. He scanned the atrium, searching every face.

The platform flashed up onto the screen above him. David stood up from the bench, picked up his suitcase and headed towards the platform. He thought of Annabel, his dad, his grandma, the deal – even the holiday to Dubai.

David was so wrapped up in his own thoughts that he didn't notice the two men reclining against the railings, didn't notice when the folder away their newspapers and began to follow him. He didn't notice the taller of the two men reach for his phone.

"He just walked past us. He won't make it to Manchester." The man said, in gravelly tones. After a pause, he continued, "Don't worry, Jefe. Everything is under control."

5

As the train pulled out of Euston, David pulled his jacket around him. The air-conditioning in the carriage a little too efficient against the late summer heat. He pulled out his paper and turned to the back for the sports pages.

The train conductor announced the stops before Manchester and David's stomach growled. Amongst the chaos so far today he had forgotten about lunch. He folded his paper onto the table in front of him, grabbed his wallet from the bag and headed for the buffet cart.

David made his way through the carriage and noticed two men sitting together on the left-hand side. He had the nagging feeling that he had seen them both before but couldn't pinpoint exactly where. Before he could think much more about it, one of the men looked up from their conversation and fixed David with a stare which soon convinced him to move on.

David leaned against the counter of the buffet carriage, analysing his options. He settled on a soggy looking ham and cheese sandwich and a water. No more coffee. His anxiety was already peaking.

He gazed out of the window at the scenery, marvelling at how different London was to the rest of England. It was almost a different world.

Soon, rolling hills and green pastures would be speeding past the window, the odd crop of houses jutting out of the landscape. These villages could likely trace their history through hundreds of years. There had been improvements, expansions, but the heart of the communities remained. It felt a long way from the urban brick-forest of London.

David had once had a fascinating conversation with a friend about the connections between the railway system and the slave trade. The railways had been developed using money earned from the long legacy of Britain's slave trade, and up until 2015 some of the public's tax money was still going towards compensating slave owners who lost their assets when slavery had been abolished.

Britain's dark history was far from common knowledge in England, and certainly had not been taught in history lessons. People seemed to celebrate Britain for eventually condemning and eradicating the industry. They seem to forget that it was Britain who established it in the first place, expanded it and used it as the basis for their now fallen empire. Of course, there were some who wouldn't consider the empire fallen, despite evidence to the contrary. David hated the 'Little Britain' mentality of some of his fellow countrymen. His mother's generation had done their best to move past the horrors of Germany under Nazi rule, some

Brits seemed intent on reliving the atrocities of the Empire and draping it in bunting.

David made his way back to his own carriage. The men he had seen earlier were no longer in their seats. Suddenly it dawned on David. They were the men from the park. Dread plunged into his stomach. A strong hand grabbed his shoulder and his flight response kicked in, but before he could run down the aisle, the hand pulled him around. A well-built, bald man peered down at him in an awkward attempt to look friendly.

"Hola, David," the man said, in a strange accent, not quite Spanish. "How are you? On your way to Manchester?"

David felt uneasy, "Who are you and why are you following me? I saw you and your mate in the park this morning. What do you want from me?" he was surprised at how bold he'd been in answering.

"It doesn't matter who I am. I am just here to give you my Jefe's message and his well wishes," he said, the corners of his mouth curling upwards, baring a row of crooked teeth in a vicious smile that didn't reach his eyes.

David was unable to meet the man's gaze. His eyes landed on the hand still clasped to his shoulder, and the tattoo on the well-muscled forearm. A snake wrapped around an axe, with the letters "ETA."

"But where are my manners? You asked about me. I am from Bilbao. I've spent ten years of my life in prison." His partner stayed silent the whole time, though matched the first man's grin. His gold tooth glistened as it caught the overhead light.

"W-what for?" David asked, immediately regretting the question. It sounded stupid, childish… and he wasn't sure he wanted to hear the answer.

"I did the right thing, and I would do it again," the man's face was stern, his eyes steely and faraway for a moment.

David began to sweat; he urgently scanned the carriage to find a way out or even just spot another person who may bear witness to his eventual murder. The second man was walking towards them. He could hear him on the phone, speaking in a language David had never heard before.

"I think you've got the wrong guy," said David, desperately trying to save himself but he knew they were looking for him.

The tall, tattooed ex-prisoner spoke again, "We hope your father and grandmother are well. Have you talked to them recently?"

The colour drained from David's face as the man finally released David's shoulder from his firm grip.

David wasn't sure how to respond.

"They are none of your business," he said, less sure of himself now. "Don't bring them into this."

"That's good to know," he glanced at his partner, "So I guess it's also not our business what Jose and William are up to in your office right now? You know David, I've heard you're a smart boy. That must mean you understand that your actions have consequences."

The other man finally interjected, "Let us give you some useful advice. Leave the train before it arrives in Manchester." The men turned together and began walking down the carriage.

The tattooed man made a phone call.

"Jefe, the job is done."

"Well done. Let me know when he leaves the train and you've got him. We will take care of his player."

"Will do Jefe. Don't worry."

6

Joska forced one eye open through the pain in her head. Fortunately, the blacked-out windows of the car diminished the harsh morning light.

It took her several moments to collect her thoughts. She didn't recognise this car. She was alone in the back, in her pyjamas. There was a man up front, driving, who she didn't recognise. At least from the back of his bald head.

She tried to piece together what had happened but couldn't remember much past the conversation with her dad before he'd flown to England.

There had been someone there, someone behind her in the mirror. Joska looked at her reflection in the window, checking for signs of injury, but could find none. She rubbed her hands over her face and neck, finding a small bump on the side of her neck. Had they injected her with something? Is that why she felt so rough?

"Where am I?" she asked, not really directing the question at anyone, just giving voice to the questions racing through her head.

The driver's eyes flicked to the rear-view mirror, but then refocused on the road ahead without saying anything.

"Hello?" Joska said, deliberately trying to get his attention now. He didn't look back this time. "Hello? Who the fuck are you? Where the fuck am I?" the reality of her situation was dawning on her as the car continued its journey. Joska looked out the window, trying to answer her own questions. They were driving on a single lane highway, a stone wall separating pastureland from the road. Several tired-looking horses stood grazing, not even looking up as the car swept past.

Beyond the fields lay a copse of trees and behind that, far in the distance the skyline rose and fell as the impossibly high tops of the Basque mountains climbed up into the heavens.

The morning sun had risen and was casting a hazy light through the cloud cover. In normal circumstances, conditions would be perfect for a long day on the beach or a walk in the hills. She imagined the smell of the earth warming up around her as she set herself up for the day, finding a quiet spot to lay down her blanket, read her book. Forget about her problems – about her mother – for a while.

Joska considered trying to talk to the driver again but didn't anticipate any response. He maintained his speed, rolling through the winding lanes that took them up into the mountains. His eyes barely moved from the road ahead. Instead, Joska tried to make herself comfortable, which was harder than it seemed with her hands tied together in her lap.

She gradually manoeuvred herself so that she was able to lay down across the back seat and turned to face the back of the seat. She wasn't tired, the adrenaline that coursed through her ensured that, but she thought that it might work in her favour to feign a casual demeanour. If they thought that being bundled into a blacked-out SUV first thing in the morning didn't faze her, perhaps they'd go easy on her. Think she was too tough a nut to crack.

As she lay down on her side, she felt an uncomfortable sensation in her bra. Her phone. She had slipped it into her bra as she had made coffee and they'd taken her before she'd taken her clothes off to shower. She imagined that because she was only in her pyjamas, they hadn't bothered to search her. No pockets.

Her heart raced. She could put a stop to this before it had even begun.

Joska brought her bound hands up to her chest, curled up her knees into a foetal position and extended her fingers, working them inside the collar of her t-shirt and into the cup of her bra where the phone was.

She teased out the device and held it as close as possible to her face as she turned down the screen brightness and switched on silent mode. The last thing she wanted was the phone blazing out light and noise as she tried to call for help.

She could no longer see the driver but could feel the car still winding as it rose. She knew these hills, had spent time here with her father as a kid, knew the narrow lanes that could barely take two cars, let alone the vast array of haulage vehicles and tourist coaches full of hikers that seemed to always be clogging up the road. The driver would be distracted by the road, focusing on not being pushed over the crash barrier that was all that was stopping them from careening into the valley below.

She opened up her messaging app and pulled up her dad's chat. She typed quickly.

SOS need help emergency

And then shared her live location. The link would work for an hour, as long as her battery lasted out. Now she just had to wait. Her dad would see the text. He was away, but he could call the police. Or maybe he'd call up some of his old friends. The ones who had provided security for the family for a while. The ones she had learned not to ask about their pasts.

The car slowed and pulled over. Joska wedged the phone in the gap between the car seats and closed her eyes, slowing her breath, relaxing her body as much as possible.

When the car was at a standstill, Joska heard the driver unclip his seatbelt and open the door, the soft ping of the seatbelt alarm bleating rhythmically as she followed the sound of his shoes crunching on the dirt road towards the back of the car.

She maintained a steady breath. They must have arrived at wherever they were going. She was hopefully about to get a bit more information on where she was. More importantly why she was there.

The door by Joska's head clunked open and without a word, the driver placed both hands on her shoulders and pulled her upright. He maintained his silence, though avoided looking at her, his eyes were fixed to the seat where she'd just laid her head. His hands swept over the seat fabric until he found what he was looking for. He grasped the phone and looked at her. He was smiling. His eyes were not full of the hatred Joska expected, but pity.

"Bad choice, girl." He moved over to the side of the road and stopped for a moment, his eyes scanning the horizon. He looked around him, checking for any signs of movement, any signs someone might be watching. The last thing he needed was some backwater farmer acting as a witness. Satisfied, he cocked his arm back and threw the phone as far as he could out into the valley below.

The man turned, closed the rear door and moved round to the driver's side. He slumped into his chair, closed the door, and moved off again up the mountain.

7

Ander checked his messages as he waited in the customs line. There was one from Parezzi, the chief scout at AC Milan, Marco's former club. The deal from Sevilla to AC Milan was off.

Useless scouts, he thought. All they do is watch games from VIP lounges and stay in luxury hotels. They're powerless.

Ander shook himself out of his disappointment and held his head high. There was nothing else he could do. His brother was no longer involved there. With that out the way, now he could focus solely on this deal.

He had to get Miller scared off. He was trying to push his German player into the club ahead of Ander. He wouldn't allow himself to be beaten by a lawyer. They had no place in football. And anyway, one player did not make a career. One deal did not get you invited to The Table.

I will teach him a lesson. He's made the mistake of trying to interfere with my business.

"What's the purpose of your visit?" a bored man in uniform beckoned him to step forward.

Ander had drifted and hadn't realised he'd reached the front of border control. He flapped about in his backpack searching for his passport. For a brief moment he was concerned that his Basque friends on the train had been picked up.

"I am visiting my brother who lives here," he said, overly formal.

The officer raised an eyebrow as he glanced at Ander's passport, "You've been here over twenty times in the last twelve months. You must love your brother a lot," he paused, "Oh, actually, wait a second," he looked up from his desk with a hint of excitement etched onto his previously blank expression, "Are you related to Marco Anaia?"

"Yes, I am, sir. He's my younger brother," Ander sighed, deferential now, just wanting to make it through customs with limited fuss. Relieved that his earlier anxiety was now not a threat, he resigned as he braced himself for the inevitable bombardment.

"Oh, mate! We all love him; the whole city loves him! Even City fans!" he exclaimed in adoration, "Massive respect."

Ander loved his brother but hated the adulation Marco received. It wasn't just fans. His family were always reminding Ander how successful his brother was, how handsome, how gracious.

"Thank you," Ander replied, plastering a smile across his face. "I'll let him know. But I really do have to go now. I am in a rush," He took back his passport and moved past the desk without looking back.

"Tell him we all love him," the officer shouted after him, "and that he should sign that new deal, stay with us, become a true legend!"

As Ander walked off, raising a dismissive hand in goodbye to the border guard, the man stepped out of his booth. He leaned over to his colleague.

"Phil, I just need a quick refreshment break."

Phil nodded, not looking up at his colleague, and waved the next person in the line forward to his desk. The guard moved away towards the toilets, one hand in his pocket, turning his mobile phone over in his hand.

He found an empty stall and pulled out the handset firing off a text message to an unsaved number.

Ander Anaia arriving at Manchester. Didn't look happy.

He immediately saw the blue ticks, the message had been received. A reply came back almost instantly.

Great, thx. Legend. I'll stick payment in usual account.

The border guard smiled and pocketed his handset, thinking of the takeaway he'd be buying tonight.

As he walked towards the cab rank, Ander made a mental checklist of the people he needed to speak with to get this deal over the line. Number one was Marco, but that was the easy part. He was reluctant to admit to himself that he knew all-too-well that he was heavily reliant upon one person to help him make this deal happen successfully.

He had faith in his brother. He knew he could rely on him to help his older brother in this time of need.

But there was also Andoni, and Aitor who hated him. It wouldn't surprise Ander if Aitor tried to scupper the deal today.

It felt as if everyone was working against him, the scouts, the media, and to his surprise, some people in the management.

He didn't see how that was possible. Marco had surrounded himself with people from the old country. His confidantes at the club were all Basque. The thought that they had lost their values by having lived amidst the strange, selfish British culture for so long shamed Ander.

And then there was Miller and his player from Germany. Well, that was one problem he'd already solved.

Ander approached the cab at the front of a snaking line of taxis.

"Good morning, Wilmslow?" he asked as the driver wound down the passenger window.

"Yes mate, no worries. Need a hand with your bag?"

Ander declined and got into the back seat with his luggage next to him. He never understood the reason for asking the cab driver where they can take you before jumping in. In any other country, you would tell the driver after you get into the cab.

Ander didn't actually like the Black Cab drivers that much. They were different from other taxi drivers he had experienced around the world. They were arrogant and unfriendly. They demanded cash, despite having a card machine, no doubt making a lot of money without paying their due taxes.

His mind refocused on what was important, the deal. If this all went off, and he secured his place at The Table, he would gain access to privileges most agents couldn't dream of. A seat at The Table meant you could place your players wherever you wanted, set your price. Ander ignored the other side of what they did. He wasn't interested.

He looked out of the window. He was getting close to his brother's house.

8

David's mind raced as he stood, silent. His legs felt heavy, a bead of sweat ran down his face.

As he finally regained some bodily feeling, he stumbled back to his seat and desperately dialled his dad's number. No answer. He tried the landline. No answer. He shifted in his seat, anxiously flicking between screens on his phone. He called Jose.

"Either you are missing us already or you're making sure we are still in the office?" Jose said as he answered.

"Look, Jose," David said, not able to match Jose's mood, "Two seriously nasty looking guys have just come up to me on the train. They threatened me; told me to walk away from the deal, or something might happen to my dad and grandma or to both of you."

There was a silence on the other end.

"Jose, are you still there?"

"Yes," said Jose, his previous lightness lost. David's heart was beating fast as he scanned the carriage for the men.

"Look mate, I don't want you or William in any danger. Or my dad and grandma. I can't take that risk. I think these guys must have been following me for a while. I didn't tell you earlier, but you know when I came back from lunch – it was these guys who'd spooked me. They approached me in the park. They looked so sketchy that I just completely ignored them. Turned and ran, actually."

"These men," Jose finally said, his voice calm, measured. David knew it was the right thing to call Jose. "What did they look like?"

"Like people you don't want to mess with," said David, "One had this tattoo on his arm – a snake wrapped around an axe, with ETA underneath. Wasn't there that Basque separatist group? I thought they'd called it quits years ago?"

The phone crackled, and David cursed the terrible mobile signal. Jose cleared his throat, "Yes, they laid down arms. But that doesn't mean they've disappeared. These guys can be very dangerous, David." David was about to thank Jose for pointing out the obvious when Jose jumped back in. "Shit, I just remembered. Do you know how Marco and Ander Anaia's dad died?"

"Enlighten me." David said, thinking it was strange he'd never heard of it. It seemed like a story the British press would have delighted in revealing all about.

"He hung himself in prison five years into his sentence. He was put in prison for being a part of an ETA terrorist attack. He always denied it but was jailed for life. I bet the guys who confronted you on the train knew Ander's dad. Maybe they feel like they owe his sons a favour... maybe he's using them to get to you?"

"I'm just going to do what they say – I can't risk putting anyone in danger." David said.

Jose was shocked, "No, Amigo. You will not leave the train," he said, "I don't think they will harm you or us. They just want to throw you off the deal. It's scare tactics. They wouldn't get away with anything more. Don't leave the train. Patrick is arriving at Manchester airport; you can't leave him stranded. You should call Aitor and tell him what's going on. See what he thinks about it all. He's Basque, like the Anaia brothers. He might be able to help you out."

David was hesitant, "I'm not sure, mate. I need to talk to my dad first. I need to know that he and gran are fine."

"Sure, amigo. But don't worry about us. We can take care of ourselves. Let us know if you need anything."

David was encouraged by Jose's nonchalance. "If anything happens to me then all I ask is that you two carry the deal through yourselves. Get in contact with Patrick and make sure it happens. If this really is Anaia, then we can't let him win."

He tried to ring his dad again but still couldn't get an answer. Why of all days is today the day his dad won't answer?

He checked his watch. Patrick must be at the airport in Düsseldorf by now. He hadn't talked to him since last night. He called him and the phone was answered before the first ring had ended.

"Hi David! How are you doing?" He sounded excited, "You must be on your way to Manchester?"

"I'm halfway there. You're at the airport, right? Your flight must be soon," David tried his best to stay professional.

"I'm already at the gate, just can't wait to get onto the plane."

David couldn't help but imagine how much more grateful Patrick would be if he knew what he was going through to get this deal for him. Though David would never tell him, he probably wouldn't believe it anyway.

"You'll pay me back when you become a star, that's all I ask for in return. You will need to fight hard and stay focused, keep doing what you're doing. Our journey is just starting; we will have plenty of opportunity to celebrate together during your career. I can assure you of that."

David could sense Patrick's smile through the phone, "I'm already looking forward to those times." David could hear the boarding announcement through the phone. "Look, David, I'll see you later. Are we at the same hotel?"

"The club will send a driver to pick you up from the airport. I'll be waiting for you at the hotel. Safe flight."

As David reached to put his phone back in his pocket the screen lit up with a message.

Don't leave your seat until you arrive in Manchester. I will explain later when you arrive. I think you might be being followed. I will be at the station. Ax

And then he heard the scream.

9

The Eagle's codename came from her predatorial instinct and her solitary existence. She had first made a name for herself in Afghanistan and Iraq where she had completed near-impossible operations, assigned to her after the Americans had failed them repeatedly.

She was unique in her solo approach. She never worked as part of a team, steadfastly holding her belief that if she was alone, it was only her who could make a mistake. Her lone-wolf success had led to foreign intelligent services affectionately dubbing her the female James Bond. No one ever suspected a woman to be the deadliest killer in the room. Only a handful of people inside the Secret Service knew her real identity.

Her success was unquestioned, but her attitude had changed. After her last deployment in Iraq, she had started to question the reason for the war.

It was clear there were no signs of any weapons of mass destruction like the Western governments had suggested. She had spent many a night staring up at the starry sky from her uncomfortable camping bed, questioning what was going on.

She felt lied to. She started to question whether MI6 was actually serving the British people.

The system had changed. She wasn't making her homeland a safer place. She was serving the rich and powerful establishment and protecting their global interests.

Then and there, lying in the middle of the Iraqi desert, The Eagle had made up her mind. She couldn't be a part of their game anymore.

So, she had gone 'dark'. Started working private jobs where the morals were as questionable as the governments, but at least the criminals were honest about their intentions. And they paid better. Twice the money, half the work.

The Eagle sat three seats behind David, watching him carefully. She felt the adrenaline in her blood and the familiar warm fuzz of her heart beating fast. She was ready to kill. She knew the feeling; she had felt it countless times before.

The train started moving and she got up slowly from her seat and walked, calm and composed, towards the back carriages.

She saw the two Basques sitting on the left-hand side of the penultimate carriage. Both men were taking the opportunity for a short siesta before the opportunity to make good on their threats later on. A teenage couple sat on the seats next to them, oblivious to the danger they were in such proximity to.

The conductor announced the next station and passengers began to move around, preoccupied by finding their suitcases, dog-earing their novels and stuffing half-eaten sandwiches into their backpacks. The Eagle attracted no suspicion.

The carriage was crowded, and a group of people had gathered by the doors as the train rolled into the station, ready to leave the moment the doors opened. The Basques seemed content in their dreams. Both had half-finished bottles of beer on the table in front of them.

How sad, she thought sarcastically, they won't finish their last beer.

She calmly took the empty seat behind the men and pulled her pistol from her belt. It was a vintage, iconic Welrod. A British bolt-action, magazine-fed, suppressed pistol which had been developed by British Major Hugh Reeves at the legendary SOE Station IX. She had inherited it from her grandfather.

It was old-fashioned but very effective and exceptionally quiet. She had altered it slightly in order to make it even quieter than even the most silenced modern weapon. It had been a talisman that kept her safe through every deployment. She maintained it obsessively and wouldn't go anywhere without it.

As the doors opened, and passengers began alighting – fumbling with cases, avoiding the passengers waiting on the platform – she checked her surroundings one final time. She fired two shots in quick succession from the Welrod through the backs of the chairs in front of her, the slugs swiftly entering the necks of her targets. The clamour of the changeover of passengers helped mask the soft put of the rounds discharging from the pistol.

The two men slumped in their chairs as the bullets destroyed their central nervous system. One of the men fell over to lay across the seat next to him. As the blood started to flow from the wounds, The Eagle began to move back towards the door of the carriage, pulling her hood over the cap that was already lowered over her face. She walked outside the station and glanced around, allowing herself to break into a slight smile as she walked towards the main street.

***

The buzzing of a phone disturbed the silence of the room. A heavy-set man who had been standing sentry by the door, his face placid, the promise of violence rippling beneath his tailored clothes, moved to pick it up.

He placed the phone to his ear to hear the confirmation the room's inhabitants had been waiting for before. He removed the rear of the phone, took out the battery and SIM card and walked over to the fireplace. He felt the warmth of the fire envelope him, relaxing his taut frame, and basked in its heat as he tossed the SIM into the flames.

The rest of the room looked to him expectantly as he glanced over to the man at the centre of the room – a curt nod of his head was met by a sneer of a smile from the man. His way of acknowledging a job well done. He was enjoying this game, as were his gathered associates. Almost as much as they were enjoying the girls.

"Gentlemen," he announced to the room, "It is done. Mr. Anaia's test has truly begun. The men he sent after Miller are dispatched. I know some of you have a lot of money riding on Anaia's client signing at United but his desperation to sit at The Table is his greatest weakness, and we must ensure he deserves his seat." He smiled, knowing how hard it was to gain a seat, knowing what he had done to get his. What he had done to keep it.

"I have little doubt that he will pull out all the stops to get his deal across the line. We will all be celebrating this time tomorrow."

The man smiled to himself. Anaia would fail, of this he was certain.

10

It was less than half an hour's drive from the airport before Ander saw the cute, white sign announcing his arrival in Wilmslow.

Wilmslow was a small town and civil parish in Cheshire, located 18km South of Manchester and formed one corner of the Golden Triangle. Also called 'the footballer belt', the area had expensive houses in pleasant countryside and over the last few years, it had become a popular place for footballers, coaches and club officials from Manchester and Liverpool to find swanky houses to live in. It was the so-called 'place to be' in Northern England.

The taxi moved through the centre of Wilmslow and out towards Alderley Edge. Ander watched as the properties changed from mid-town terraces, squeezed together on dirty streets to enclosed communities of semi-detached family homes devoid of any architectural charm. No shops, no parks, just rows enclaves of identical houses with matching cars in the driveway.

As the car moved out past these housing estates, the houses changed once again. Gigantic edifices rose out of gravel driveways. Huge, ostentatious displays of wealth, with bold architectural considerations, manicured front lawns and sports cars which cost more than the average house in England littered the frontages.

The taxi pulled up in Marco's driveway and Ander asked the driver to wait for him, "I'll only be a few moments."

"I'll have to keep the meter running," said the driver, smiling at the opportunity to make money from doing nothing.

He walked up to his brother's grand entrance and rang the doorbell and waited for an answer. He had sent Marco a text last night to let him know that he would be arriving in the morning but was yet to receive a response.

His brother's wife, Maria, greeted him with a welcoming grin; "Oh, *buenos dias*, Ander. How are you? Come on in. The boys have just left for school, and I was having a coffee. Do you want one?"

Ander had always been cautious around Maria. Whilst she had always made his brother happy, he knew that she was wary of Ander's relationship with him. He felt that she had never been fully comfortable around him, especially after recent times of tension between the two brothers.

When she had first met Marco, she was a fledgling doctor who had been practicing and studying medicine. But once Marco's career had taken off, she didn't need to work to support herself or him and had changed focus to doing charitable work. She had worked on the frontline in Afghanistan with Médecins Sans Frontières, delivering emergency care to civilians caught in the crossfire between the government and the Taliban. When she found out she was pregnant, she had moved to safer work, helping with the prevention of cervical cancer in Malawi.

When the children had been born, she had recalibrated. She wanted to give them as much time as she could whilst they were young, and she missed Marco. She had handed in her notice and moved to the UK with Marco. She kept herself busy by coordinating fundraisers for the organisations she used to work for.

Ander reluctantly engaged in the usual pleasantries, "I'm well, thanks Maria. Nothing for me though thank you, I don't have long. How is everything here in England? Looks like we can expect a few days of good weather."

"Good Ander, the usual. Looking after three big boys in this house. You can imagine what that means!" she said, chuckling quietly. "How is the family in Bilbao? How's mum?" Maria asked.

"They are all well, thanks. Mum is missing the kids a lot, as you can imagine."

"She still doesn't want to come to see them in Manchester?"

"You know her, Maria; she would fret if she had to leave the village for longer than an hour. She seems content with sticking to her once-a-year visit. I think she expects you all to come more often, but I always remind her how busy Marco is," Ander left a pregnant pause. He had always been the mummy's boy whereas Marco had done his own thing from an early age. It had always been a point of tension – the more distant Marco got, the more his mother seemed to want him. Ander had never been quite sure whether it was intentional on Marco's part. Ander tried to move the conversation on to the real reason he was here, "Talking about my brother, is he not at home?"

Maria took the hint, "Oh, he left very early this morning. He told me last night that there were a few new signings and he needed to be there early enough to get on top of it all."

The reality of the situation sunk in a little further for Ander. Maria's face fell, "Is there anything I should know, Ander? Did something bad happen back in Bilbao? Is your mother okay?"

"No, no, all good Maria," as Ander realised the scare he had caused, "Everything is fine back home," he said reassuringly.

There was a brief pause, and Ander could tell Maria was weighing up whether she believed him or not.

He continued, "I don't mean to have caused you any stress, and I don't want to be rude, but I have to leave. I'm in a bit of a rush. I have a deal that I still need to finish. You know how it is. I'll catch Marco at the training ground."

Maria still seemed flustered, "Ander, please be careful. Don't put your brother in an awkward situation again," she warned, "Family is family and business is business. Please stop combining them, it doesn't help your brother."

Ander looked urgently for an excuse to leave as he recalled how angry Marco had been in January when Ander had pushed his young player out of Manchester United for another club and how he used his brother to help him, against the will of the rest of the club.

"My brother is the club, Maria!" Ander fired back, his voice rising, "He is the manager. He makes the decisions about players, who comes and who goes. Not anyone else! That was our deal when he signed here three years ago. I was the one who negotiated that for him, to ensure he had more power. And you don't know the details about the deal in January either." Ander took a quick, exasperated breath before his rant continued, "And I'm not mixing anything here. In our culture family and business go together, Maria." He stopped himself, seeing the hurt on Maria's face.

Like Ander and his brother, Maria was from Bilbao, but her parents were not Basque. They were from Madrid. Her father was a professor of medicine at the University Hospital of Basurto in Bilbao.

Her father had insisted that she learned the Basque language. As a child she questioned her father about the necessity of learning the language. He explained that "To understand a different culture you must first learn their language, Maria. Learning another language will make you wiser and stand you in good stead in the communities in which you live."

Maria gulped down the lump in her throat and spoke back softly, but stubbornly, "I might not be born a Basque like you, but I feel Basque as much as I feel Spanish. What you think will not change that. I think you should leave."

Ander didn't need any more encouragement than that and turned on his heel to leave.

As he got back into the waiting cab, his phone vibrated in his pocket. It was a message from his friends who had met David on the train. He thought it was odd that they'd sent him a link to a news item, but his curiosity got the better of him. As the page loaded, his eyes widened in horror.

DOUBLE MURDER: TWO MURDERED ON MANCHESTER TRAIN. TERROR LINK SUSPECTED

As he read the article, a notification came through from Joska. No doubt she'd reconciled with her mother. He'd catch up on that later, when he had time to think.

11

The cab took the motorway route to avoid the rush hour traffic inside Manchester. The sights out of the window seemed everchanging to Ander. There has been a lot of construction and development projects in the city carried out over the last few years that he had been visiting, and the infrastructure and appearance of the city had altered considerably. Manchester was truly living up to its reputation as the Capital of the North.

Despite this, every player that Ander had dealt with still expressed a clear preference of playing for a London club rather than in Manchester. London was the place to live. The life in London outside of football was seen to be far better for players and their families.

It was not uncommon for the players of Northern clubs to spend their days off enjoying what the capital had to offer. They would take the train or drive down in their supercars to cruise around on the Brompton Road in Knightsbridge. Often, a group of players would arrange a chartered jet or helicopter to visit the city.

"So, are you working for the Red Devils?" The driver asked in an unwelcomed attempt to strike up a conversation.

"No, I'm not." Ander responded bluntly.

The driver seemed to lose interest in Ander and began to talk about himself instead, "I am a United fan, myself. Used to go to every game back in the eighties and nineties."

"Why did you stop?" Ander asked.

Unfortunately, Ander's sarcasm didn't shine through, and the driver took the opportunity to wax lyrical. Ander rolled his eyes as the driver began a monologue.

"I've lost my passion for the club. I don't feel the connection to the team anymore. I used to go to the Cliff, chat with the players and get autographs after the game. We were even allowed to watch their training sessions. Now you can't get anywhere near Fortress Carrington. They built security walls right the way around, and then thirty-thousand trees in front of that, so that no one can get a look in. Cameras, alarms, patrols. It's like a prison." He let out an exaggerated breath.

"We felt like we were part of the team, in a way. We would follow them around the country, home and away, through all the ups and downs." His proud look diminished as he paused.

"No one cares about us anymore. True football and true United has been lost. No one I know — some that I used to sit with at every game — can afford a season ticket. Our old seats are filled with corporates, friends of the dignitaries of the club and wealthy businessmen from Asia, the Middle East and Europe." To Ander's concern, the man kept turning his head to Ander and the taxi jerked across the lane each time. "They aren't real fans, but they can pay for these expensive tickets. I'd have to work overtime to even afford a home shirt now!"

Ander laughed inwardly at the idea of this middle-aged man worrying about being able to afford a football kit. Replica kits were for children, not paunchy, sallow-skinned men.

"The stadium serves the wealthy." The cabbie continued, though Ander was glad he seemed to be keeping his eyes on the road now. "The hospitality boxes get the best views, even though half of the people in them couldn't give a toss about watching the football. They just come for the free food and drink. The pubs are the new Old Trafford for the real fans."

The driver shook his head and sighed as he turned off of the main road of traffic Ander regretted engaging with the driver. He had far more important things to worry about than a disgruntled cabbie moaning about the state of football.

"We've been left behind by the club but at least in the pubs we can still be together. The ones who loved to see their own young blood come through the academy. Kids who used to play for the badge on their shirt rather than the pay packet that comes after.

It's all a money-driven business now and we're ruled by foreign owners who have no clue about football, they just think about business and profit. Whatever happened to the values and foundations of 'the beautiful game'?"

Ander could not care less and was struggling to restrain himself; he couldn't listen anymore. The driver was showing no signs of stopping talking any time soon, so Ander zoned out and looked at his phone. Marco still hadn't replied.

He must be busy. Perhaps he had just forgotten to answer him.

Ander tried to call him, thinking it might also shut the driver up. No answer. He tried again. Same result.

Ander tried his best to reassure himself as the driver droned on in the front. He must be in a meeting, he told himself.

***

After a journey that seemed to last a lifetime, the cab arrived in Carrington and made a left turn into Isherwood Road. Halfway along the road sign changed into Birch Road. There it was, on the left-hand side he could see the high walls of the Manchester United Aon Training Complex.

The cab stopped outside the facility and the driver swivelled to face him, "Welcome to 'the Prison', sir," he announced in an exaggerated tone.

"Thanks for the ride… and the chat," Ander said, "How much?" He was waiting for the inevitable attempt of the driver to rip him off.

"Thirty is okay. I didn't turn on the meter. Otherwise, you would have ended up paying at least forty-five."

"Oh, how generous of you!", Ander said, even more sarcastically than before. "You know, we have something in common?" Ander exclaimed, his voice making his irritation obvious.

"What's that?" The cab looked at Ander with bemusement.

He gave him the cash as he got out and chuckled; "Black cab drivers and agents have the same bad reputation. Always trying to squeeze people for their money." With that he closed the door and headed towards the entrance of the training ground.

Two security guards stood at the entrance of the complex. A well-built, tower of a man stepped in front of him.

"Good morning, sir. Do you have a meeting here today?" he stood in front of Ander, blocking his path into the training complex, placing a hand in the centre of Ander's chest as Ander tried to walk past him.

"I am Ander Anaia. The brother of Marco Anaia," Ander shot back.

"Okay sir, do you have a meeting with your brother or with someone else?" the security guard was staring at the tablet he held in front of him.

After the awful cab journey and getting ripped off by the driver, Ander didn't have any patience for the petty power trip of a security guard.

"What kind of question is that? Open the gate and let me in. I just told you who I am," he pointed out arrogantly, motioning towards the grand iron gates at the entrance to the complex.

The guard stayed professional, "I'm just doing my job, sir. Do you have an appointment to see Mr. Anaia today?"

"Ask me another question and see what happens. If I'm delayed a minute further, I'll make sure you no longer have a job to do."

A second guard had been sat looking at the computer inside the small security building. She finally looked up as she heard Ander's raised voice. She leaped out of his chair and ran out of the building towards them.

"Good morning Mr. Anaia, how are you? Lovely to see you again." She paused and nodded towards the taller guard, "Sorry, my colleague is new here. Let me open the gate for you."

Ander responded with a glare in her direction.

"I'll make sure to let Marco know the hassle you've cause me this morning. Unbelievable."

As the two guards walked back inside the security hut, he listened closely to try to hear the new guard being reprimanded, being told how important Ander was. To his disappointment he only heard the phone dialling.

"Mr. Gaizka, this is security. He's just arrived sir." There was a slight delay as the guard listened to Aitor Gaizka's reply. "Very well, sir — let me know if you need us."

The second guard returned and handed Ander a guest pass with a plastic wallet and lanyard that Ander swiftly put away in the inside pocket of his suit jacket.

"I think you know the way, sir? Or would you like one of us to escort you?" asked the guard.

Without answering, Ander barged past and headed into the training ground to see his brother.

"What a strange guy. Now I understand what you were saying about no one here liking the man," said the first guard.

"Same mum, same dad but so different. Although who knows? Maybe Marco is just acting the good guy…" the second guard contemplated.

12

Joska sat in the corner of the room, feet tucked in close, hugging her knees to her chest. A shiver coursed through her as she sat there. When they had taken her, she had been wearing her pyjamas and they were not standing up well to the damp basement room. The cold seeped through the thin cotton shorts and she hugged her knees closer, rubbing her hands up and down her legs trying to get some warmth into them.

She had completely lost track of the time. It had been early morning when they took her, and it didn't seem like she had been in the car for very long. A few hours maybe. She tried to imagine a map, tried to guess where they could have reached in that time. They had been travelling up hill, so she anticipated it would be somewhere in the Sierras.

A hatch in the top of the door slid back, metal rasping, and a face appeared in the porthole.

"Food," a man said, and opened another hatch in the middle of the door. This was not the same man who had driver her here. She could only make out his eyes through the hatch, sunken and hollow with thick black rings underneath.

He passed through a tray on which was piled of food that looked like it had been assembled by a stoned teenager. A jar of peanut butter, crackers, an apple, a handful of crisps and a chocolate bar. Joska took the tray, opened the bottle of water and glugged down the whole thing without drawing breath. It was only when she had finished that panic set in: what if they'd drugged the water?

Clearly sensing the girl's panic, the man at the door reassured her.

"Relax. If they wanted you dead, we wouldn't be having this conversation." His Spanish was heavily accented, and Joska took a gamble.

"Where am I? Who are they?" she asked, though her Basque had got a little rusty since she'd been living with her mother in Barcelona.

The man laughed, but answered back in Basque, "The cost of the answer to either of those questions is not worth thinking about. Eat. Try to sleep. If your dad does as he's asked, this will all be over soon enough." With that, he closed both hatches, plunging Joska back into a twilight darkness.

The only light in the room came through a high window on the rear of the cell. She carried the tray over to the small square of light and tried to listen to see if she could hear anything outside that would indicate where she might be. But there was nothing apart from the occasional bird call, a dog barking in the far distance.

As she set about the food in front of her, she considered what the man had said. Whoever had taken her had something to do with her father. Had he got into trouble with another of his shady deals? It was the thing that had driven her parents apart – as her father had gotten more powerful in his job, he had begun to leave his morals behind him. It wouldn't be too much of a leap to consider that he might have got involved with some crooked people along the way.

But how did she come into it? Things must be pretty bad if they were willing to kidnap someone to make a point.

As she sat and thought about her predicament, the middle hatch in the door slid open again and blankets were passed through. She unfolded them and laid out a space in the corner, rolling up one of the blankets to make a pillow.

Her bladder twinged and she regretted drinking the entire bottle of water now. She knocked on the door.

"Excuse me, sir." She remained as formal as she could – he had told her she wasn't in any immediate danger, but some carefully applied charm could make this experience better until her dad did whatever these people wanted. "I need to use the bathroom."

There was a pause, and the sound of footsteps moving away along the corridor. After a few minutes, she heard the footsteps returning. They stopped outside the door and the middle hatch slid open once more. A bucket appeared

"Now," the man said, "That's enough for today. I don't want to hear anything more out of you. It would make your stay less pleasant if I had to gag you."

Joska stared at the bucket, cringing at the thought of having to use it, but pulled it through, saying nothing.

13

The impressive surroundings of the Aon training complex never failed to impress Ander. The facility boasts 108 acres of land, including a total of 14 high-tech football pitches with under-soil heating, irrigation sprinklers and drainage.

There was a low buzz of activity as the hundreds of employees navigated their way amongst the vast array of offices and speciality rooms throughout. Ander was always surprised at how calm everything seemed.

He checked his phone. It was Marco, finally replying to the message he'd sent the previous day.

Good morning, brother. On my way to the training ground. I will see you there soon.

Ander gulped down a lump in his throat. When is soon? he thought. Time was not on his side. He also held a small suspicion that his brother may be lying and was avoiding him. He just didn't know why yet.

Ander barely had a chance to think about a reply before his phone started to ring. It was his client, Markel, from

Bilbao. Ander needed no further stress; his immediate reaction was to ignore the call. He paused and reconsidered. Knowing Markel, he was probably sat with his parents too, Ander had to answer. Reluctantly, he clicked the green icon.

"Good morning, Markel," he said, through gritted teeth, "How are you, *mi hermano*?"

"I'm good Ander. I'm sitting here waiting with Mum and Dad," he confirmed Ander's intuition before barraging him with his own worries, "What's the latest? When do I fly to Manchester? The sporting director from Bilbao called us a minute ago and told us that there was still no official offer from United and that I should return to training? Journalists haven't stopped calling me, calling my dad… we have no idea what to tell them." The words were coming thick and fast, and Ander had a hard time getting a word in. Markel was clearly nervous. "Even someone from MARCA called last night. Dad tried his best to assure them that all was well and that I will be transferred to Man U. I told him not to talk to anyone from the media, but you know how it is once they have a family member on the phone. We need to be kept in the loop, Ander, we deserve to know everything as it happens."

Markel's anxiousness only worsened Ander's stress. He felt a headache brewing in the space behind his eyes.

"What have I told you about speaking to the press? And your dad?" Ander had warned them so often about the dangers of speaking to journalists, "They pretend to be your friends, Markel, but the slightest wrong move could destroy the transfer and your future." His tone was harsh, but Ander tried to keep most of his anger hidden. Really, he was talking through Markel to his father, who he assumed was listening to him on loudspeaker. Part of him longed to lose control and tell Markel's dad just how much of an idiot he had been to risk it all like this. Ander was a better professional than that. He couldn't afford to fall out with them on a day like today, he could readdress the issue in a couple of days after Markel had safely arrived in Manchester and been presented to a huge crowd of excited United fans.

Markel's father's loose lips did mean that Ander now had another problem. If this was leaked to the media earlier than appropriate, there would be trouble. He needed to call the guy at MARCA right after this phone call, head it off before any real damage was done.

MARCA was a Spanish sports media company. They were known for being the first to find out the newest gossip from the Spanish football world. Who knew what else Markel's father told them on the phone?

"Don't worry, everything is going to be fine, Markel." Ander tried his best to sound confident and unphased, "I have everything under control. These things can take time. The club is finalising other deals and then it will be your turn." In truth, Ander didn't know what was taking so long. He would know more once he'd seen Marco.

"I reckon you'll be brought over tonight or tomorrow morning for the medical and the signing. I'm just about to meet with my brother and the rest of the management team to find out more about the exact schedule. I'll pass it on to you straight away. They are just more relaxed with me because everything is already agreed and just needs to be signed. Don't worry about Bilbao either, they are worried about the money. Let me sort everything, you can just relax. Remember, I've done this hundreds of times."

Ander reiterated his point once more, "Please, just do me a favour. All of you. Don't talk to the press."

The slight pause made Ander wonder whether he'd taken too hard a tone with Markel, but soon the boy answered him. "Thanks, Ander. I trust you. I'm glad to have you. I can't wait to come over and play for your brother. Every boy from Bilbao dreams of playing for him," said Markel enthusiastically.

Ander broke into a brief smile, this was more like what he wanted to hear, "Together we will make this deal happen. I'll call you once I have more news about the transfer and your travel arrangements. Adios, Markel."

Ander ended the call and dialled in Sergio's number. Sergio had been a friend of Ander's for a while. He was a journalist for MARCA, but one that Ander could trust. He answered the phone almost instantly.

"Buenos dias Jefe. Que pasa?"

"*Buenos dias, Sergio.* I've just spoken with Markel, and he said his dad talked to someone from MARCA. Do you know anything?"

"Not to my knowledge. I'll ask around and let you know what I hear. I'll ring you back."

"Please Sergio, its vitally important. I don't want this coming out. I have enough to deal with over here in

Manchester, the last thing I need is to have an issue back in Spain."

"I'll call you Jefe," Sergio replied bluntly and hung up the phone. Ander had no choice but to trust him.

Ander sent a reply to his brother before walking through the revolving doors of the main building.

I'm here, hermano. I will talk to the other guys until you arrive. Please hurry, we have important things to discuss. Adios.

"Good morning, Ander. How are you?" sat at the reception desk was Victoria, she had been there ever since his brother became the coach of the club.

She wore heavy makeup and smelled strongly of expensive perfume. Her lips had been pumped up by doctors to the point where Ander feared they might burst. Even when she spoke, her face sat rigid, fixed by all the other work she had had done.

However, there was more to Victoria than the artificial looks and extortionate spending on cosmetic surgery. Beneath this exterior sat a highly personable woman. She knew everyone and everything, she was socially-savvy and knew when and how to talk to any person who walked through the doors. It was a subtle manipulation, and she was able to win over everyone she spoke to. She was someone that you wanted to like you as she could always help you if you needed it.

Everyone, that was, but Ander. He knew her game and didn't like it one bit, but he had to put on an act as he still couldn't help thinking that maybe his brother had lied and was in his office already.

"Good morning, Victoria," Ander beamed, "I'm good, how are you? You are looking fantastic as always." He gave her no time to reply, "Do you happen to know what time my brother arrived this morning?"

Victoria saw through Ander's empty compliments; she knew what he was after.

"I only arrived ten minutes before you Ander, so I don't know if Mr. Anaia is in yet. Let me call his office now and find out."

"No, leave it Victoria. Its fine. It's nothing important. I'll ask him myself when I see him," Ander knew she was lying to him. He tried to mask his frustration as he knew there was nothing he could do. She clearly didn't want to tell him anything about Marco's whereabouts.

"Please can you call Aitor, though, and tell him that I am on my way to his office."

"Will do, Ander," she paused as if she was looking for another excuse to stall him, "I just need to check if he is in a meeting quickly," she eventually called after Ander as he turned to leave.

Ander took a deep breath and turned to her. His face betrayed his anger as he was once more confronted with the feeling that everyone at the club this morning – his brother included – seemed to be working in tandem against him.

Ander leaned over the desk until his face was very close to Victoria's and talked quietly so that he was not audible to any cameras or microphones that could record what he said.

"Listen carefully to me, Victoria," his voice was hushed but his tone harsh, "All the fillers in the world couldn't cover up how ugly you are when you lie. I could see from your eyes that you lied to me about Marco. My own brother! It's not the first time you've done it either." Victoria stared at him blankly.

"I've had enough of being treated like a stranger! I'm not just going to sit here like a moron until my brother arrives. Do you think I'm stupid? Stop playing games with me. I know that you have your orders but you're a smart girl, just help me out," he was verging on begging her before he began to target her personally. "Call Aitor right now and tell him I am coming."

Without saying a word, Victoria picked up the phone and called Aitor.

"I've really had enough of it now," Ander continued as the phone rung, "Show me some respect and be honest with me and we'll have no problems in the future."

Victoria spoke briefly and put the phone down, glancing up to Ander, on the verge of tears.

"He's expecting you, Ander," she said softly.

"Well done, that's a good start Victoria." He walked off with an air of defiance, proud of getting his way, proud of having brought Victoria down a peg. She was nothing more than a trumped-up receptionist. How dare she try to control him in such a way. His blood was in this club.

As soon as Ander was out of earshot, Victoria picked up the phone and dialled Marco's number. The call connected, and a smile crept across her face as Marco greeted her warmly.

"He's been here for less than five minutes and has already threatened me and talked to me like shit. I hate him, Marco – I don't know how you put up with him"

Marco could sense the upset in her voice. Part of being a great football manager was knowing individuals well and knowing when and how to comfort and support them.

"Don't take his words seriously, Victoria. You know how he is. You do not deserve to be treated like that by anyone, let alone my brother. I will be there soon and will have a stern word with him. You are stronger than his petty words, just try your best to let it go."

"If it wasn't for you, I would tell him exactly what I think about him."

"I don't blame you," Marco laughed, "But be careful, Victoria. He has people inside the club, anything you say may come back to him at some point. Don't talk to anyone except me about my brother please. It's for the best. Do you understand?"

"Don't worry Marco," she said with a sigh, shaking her head at the fact someone could talk to her in such a manner and get away with it. "I miss you," she added quietly.

"Bye, Victoria."

"Bye, Marco."

14

The main building for the first team at the Aon training ground had two levels. The ground floor was like a luxurious, high-end spa with a rehabilitation centre that included a huge gym, indoor running tracks, a rehabilitation training hall, squash and basketball courts, specialized weight rooms, a twenty-five-meter swimming pool, remedial hydrotherapy pools, yoga rooms, a spa pool, a jacuzzi, underwater treadmills, a sauna and a few steam rooms for good measure. They even had Vitamin-D intensive sun beds and seven team changing rooms.

The top floor housed the head doctor's office, the chief physio's office, classrooms, and several conference rooms. There was also a gourmet restaurant with a capacity of over 100 people and a lavish players' lounge, including games rooms stacked to the brim with the latest consoles, table tennis and snooker tables, and an elevated, covered viewing gallery overlooking the outdoor pitches.

Marco's office was on the top floor, beside his personal assistant's office. There was also the assistant manager's office, coaches' offices and the impressive, cinema-like match and opposition analysis suite.

Recently, the sporting director, Aitor Gaizka, had settled himself into the assistant manager's office next to Marco. The actual assistant manager had been displaced and was forced to share a room with one of the coaches instead.

Aitor had enough authority within the club to choose where his office was, and he didn't want it to be in one of the executive rooms downstairs. The real action happened upstairs, this was where any important or influential people came in and out to see the manager. He had wanted to be close to Marco, and the drama, since he had arrived at the club. Before Marco himself had even settled in, Aitor had moved in next to him.

"It's better for us to be close so it is easier for us to discuss anything important," he had told Marco, "This way we don't need to walk around this maze to find each other. Together, we need to get this club to the pinnacle in three years. The owners demand success."

"That's a brilliant idea," Marco had said, lying through a forced smile. He had disliked Aitor since they had crossed paths for the first time in Bilbao, eight years ago.

Marco had left the club to manage AC Milan. During the five years that he was there, their relationship was reduced to the occasional Christmas and birthday message. He had thought he would never have to deal with Aitor again. He had been wrong, now they were back together and closer than ever. One room apart in fact.

Aitor had been pleased, fooled by Marco's lie, "Very well hombre. I'm looking forward to enjoying all the success we have here with you."

Marco had been convinced to join United by the American, Texas-born owners and the CEO who he had known from his playing career in Bilbao.

The legendary captain of Bilbao, Andoni Andoni, had been the CEO of Manchester United for five years. Both the owners and Andoni gave everything they could think of until, eventually, they persuaded Marco and his family to accept the offer from the club.

Over time, it seemed that the important people in Manchester United all seemed to come from the same Basque circle.

Aitor was close to Andoni too because their families had been brought together by marriage. Aitor had married Andoni's sister, Anna.

Since then, Aitor had been protected by the family umbrella of Andoni. This meant that it wasn't easy for Marco to work with Aitor when it came to recruitment.

He knew that Aitor would be at the club as long as Andoni remained as CEO. The two came as a pair. Any disagreement with Aitor would lead back to Andoni who would defend his brother-in-law, regardless of whether he was right or wrong.

Marco was an intelligent man; he knew he needed to keep a good relationship with both of them if he ever wanted to get his own way. It was why Ander had tried so hard to negotiate a deal that gave his brother sufficient authority. Asserting that authority was a different matter, sometimes.

Ander walked up the stairs and headed along the corridor towards Aitor's office. He passed the big office area designated to marketing and branding and glanced through the windows of the office. He marvelled at the impressive, military-like operation.

Despite the struggles on the pitch over the last few years, the club was still a commercial powerhouse and, indisputably, the biggest English football brand in the world.

Ander passed his brother's office, half expecting to see Marco sat inside. To his surprise, no one was in there, perhaps Victoria had been telling the truth after all. He felt a small twinge of remorse.

He continued to the polished hardwood door of the office next door, taking a deep breath, and raised his arm to knock. He was startled as Aitor flung it open before him.

"Ander! Come in, I was expecting you. Marco just told me you were due to arrive today. Victoria just rang." Aitor's characteristic husky baritone filled the cavernous space around them. His most recently developed habit of smoking expensive Cuban cigars had done no favours to his throaty tone. He had an unsettling habit of licking his bushy moustache between sentences.

The office was fitting for Aitor. It was a small, cosy room that smelt strongly of single malt and cigar smoke. The walls hung with a range of awards, certificates, and photos of Aitor with famous celebrities and sports stars. Some small bits of silverware were sat in an orderly fashion on a shelf, next to a supremely well stocked bar.

Aitor was smaller than Ander and rounder. He looked up at Ander with a disconcerting, slightly menacing, grin. Altogether it gave him the appearance of some sort of despot, and he carried the aura of someone who knew he had a lot of power.

"Good morning Aitor," Ander replied, perhaps a little too loudly. His confidence was waning, in the face of the unusual reception at the club this morning. "How are you doing? You must be busy. Last two days of the transfer window!"

"I'm always busy, Ander, you know that. I'm sure this ridiculous change to the timings of the transfer window will be changed back to the old system next summer. It's completely limiting our opportunities and disadvantages us against our European competition."

"I see," Ander couldn't care less about Aitor's worries, he just wanted to get his own deal done. "Is that the excuse you're going to use for not signing my player then?"

Like his brother, Ander didn't particularly like Aitor either, but in this case the feelings were mutual. Aitor always prepared for a bit of conflict and disagreement when Ander came into the office.

"Ander, what are you talking about?" he said, disgruntled, "Your player is not a Manchester United player. At least not yet. I told you that we can revisit the offer and reconsider him next year."

This was exactly what Ander didn't want to hear, he felt his cheeks warming. "Do not try to tell me anything about my players. I don't care what kind of position you have here, you are not entitled to decide which players come in and out of this team. That's Marco's decision and only his! I'll let you know what he says and then your job is to put the deal on paper, understood?" Ander couldn't help himself, he wasn't ready to deal with Aitor trying to power grab and make himself feel influential. "Do not tell me Markel is not a Manchester United player, because he is. I have six more players here, four of them playing first team football and two more on loan to Germany. If it wasn't for me and my clients, you would be eight players short next season!"

He was starting to boast now, perhaps pushing it too far, but Ander was using this opportunity to vent at Aitor knowing that there was little further damage to be done to their relationship.

"Do you really think I would offer you a player that isn't good enough to be here? Are you trying to tell me that I don't know what I'm doing?"

There was a short silence as Ander tried to get his breath back and calm himself. He never appreciated his abilities and players being questioned, especially not on a day like this.

Ander's face lit up with anger again.

"How dare you. I give back Aitor. To my people. I take care of them. I am not like you. I think about my people and not about myself. Do not accuse me of greed. Amigo, "

Ander took another breath, "Markel is more than good enough to play here. He is the best player in the whole Basque region. They don't let any random 18-year-old start for a La Liga first team; you have to be pretty special. He is a future star, why wouldn't you want him here to help United achieve the success you are after?"

Ander had settled into his rant and wasn't going to stop, but interrupted by Aitor's assistant looking into the office, asking if someone wanted a drink. She looked uneasy as she gauged the tense atmosphere in the room. Both men shot back the same order, "Double Espresso," and the woman swiftly exited the room.

Ander calmed himself and gazed at the man opposite him. He was a man with a habit for good food and good wine, which was reflected in the stomach that hung some way over his belt.

Aitor seized the opportunity to break the tension and spoke with the softest tone he could muster. "Look, Ander, listen to me. I understand you're disappointed, but this is not just my opinion. Everyone else in the club shares it. We really don't think he is good enough. We are playing in the Champions League this season and we need more experienced players."

Ander had a face like thunder, he was on the edge of losing control of this before he'd even had a chance to speak to Marco. "So, this German player you want to get instead is more experienced?" He managed to ask solemnly.

"I cannot and will not discuss every player we may or may not be bringing to the club. I will reiterate, it is not my decision alone. The scouting department, the Head of football and the coaching staff thinks the same, and of course your brother who has all that power!" he added, immediately regretting his sarcasm as he looked up at Ander's face.

"What the hell is going on here Aitor. Don't give me that bullshit talk you give to the other agents. Where is your respect?" Ander tried to appeal to the common Basque grounds they shared, "Have you all forgotten about your past, your history, your people? You've lived away from your heart's home for so long you guys are losing your roots. Can't you see how the other groups work together? Why do we not do the same?"

Aitor sat silently, his face expressionless as he let Ander's rant wash over him.

"Ander you are living in a fantasy world, it doesn't work like that anymore. Football is a global business; it's not about helping your people. We are representing the rich businesspeople who own this club. We are working for them. We don't represent the Basque people over here. You shouldn't mix these things up."

Ander shook his head in disbelief, "I haven't mixed anything. You guys have lost it completely. The owners have given you this position and you are not using it to support our people, like others are doing for theirs. I am not telling you to sign a bad player. It's really very simple, am telling you to sign the Under-21 Spanish National Team captain instead of the German Under-21 Captain. My player is Basque. Don't you get it?"

Aitor realised he was never going to get Ander to see his point of view, "Please, Ander, I don't want to argue with you. The decision has been made"

"You won't have to argue if you support your own people, sign a future superstar and not go for Miller's German player," Ander said, sneering as he once more pushed his agenda onto Aitor.

"I don't think you should combine family and business either, Ander." Ander was growing increasingly frustrated as Aitor met each of his rants in a calm, measured tone. "You are putting your brother in a very difficult position, and not for the first time either. He has his own job to do, he is trying to do the best for the team; you are not helping him right now. You are making it harder than it needs to be. You talk about supporting your people… why don't you support your brother and stop adding to his problems?"

Ander did not appreciate the lecture. "Wow, not mixing family and business? Look who is saying that. You seem to have forgotten that the only reason you are here is your brother-in-law. If it weren't for him, you'd be somewhere in Bilbao working for a reserve team."

"You can't judge me Ander: I really don't care what you think about me," Aitor tried to hide the offence Ander had caused him, "I work for this club, and I have instructions to follow to ensure that we are successful. You are not my boss, and I will not let you tell me what I should and should not do."

"We will see Aitor," Ander's ego had taken a hit. "You sneaky bastard. You will not influence my brother. You are my enemy, and I will treat you as you deserve." He stood up from his chair and swivelled towards the door to leave.

"No one can influence me, Ander," said Marco Anaia, stood at the doorway with Andoni Andoni. Ander's face, puce from his argument with Aitor, lost all colour; shocked at the sudden appearance of his brother and Andoni, adrenaline had kicked in and he felt his stomach lurch and his knees turn to jelly.

"Marco, brother," Ander scrambled for words, "We were just discussing my player from Bilbao."

Marco gave him a stern look, "Let's go outside Ander. I need to talk to you."

"Should I join you guys?" asked Andoni.

"No, Andoni. I would like to talk to my brother in private, please."

Before Ander even addressed Andoni's presence, he was marched out of the office by his brother.

"Why are we not going to your room?" asked Ander, anxiously.

Marco looked worryingly serious, "We need to leave the building before we start talking. Things have changed over here brother. I will explain once we are out there but let's keep it private."

15

The train had pulled into Stockport. It was the last station before Manchester Piccadilly. Squads of police were stood along the platform, which was empty except for them.

The woman who David had heard scream had fainted and fallen back onto the man who'd been following her down the train aisle. The commotion that surrounded trying to revive the woman meant that the source of her terror – the two dead men – had been ignored until the train had pulled out of Wilmslow.

A crowd had gathered around the fainted woman, and the conductor had worked her way down the train and was administering first aid. The man the woman had fallen back onto had managed to extricate him from the tangle of limbs and luggage and had sat on the closest seat to catch his breath.

He found it odd that the two men sat in the bank of seats had managed to stay asleep during the whole commotion. Looking at them, though, they looked like they'd had a hard life. Covered in tattoos, heads shorn, one had a deep scar running from above his eyebrow past his cheekbone down to his jaw. They were both slumped over on the seats next to them. Drugs, the man thought to himself, and left the men to sleep it off.

He felt movement behind him, and saw the gathered crowd disburse slightly.

"Okay, people – let's make some space. Give her room to breathe." The conductor was instructing people to step back. He saw the woman who had fainted onto him sat up now, looking about her, her eyes blinking like some sort of animal, trying to take in her surroundings. Why was she on the floor?

The man saw the moment it clicked, the woman remembering what had caused her to scream.

"Please," she said, to no one in particular, "Those men… they're … they're dead."

The man turned back to look at the sleeping men. He took the man with the scar by the shoulder.

"Excuse me, mate?" he shook him, but the man didn't respond "Mate? Are you alright?" Still no response, the man's stomach dropped, and he instinctively reached his hand to the man's throat. No pulse. He jumped back, looking at the conductor.

"Call the police. We need to get everyone out of here, now."

***

David still couldn't reach his dad or his grandma and since his run in with the thugs, he was worried about Jose and William back in London too.

The hedges and buildings became less blurry, the train was slowing as it neared the platform. As much as he wanted and needed this deal, he couldn't put his friends, his family, himself at risk.

The Tannoy announced Stockport as the next station and kindly reminded him to take his belongings. He decided his safest option was to get off and call Annabel then decide what to do from there.

As he got up from his seat, he heard a piercing scream coming from the carriage behind. It was quickly followed by more screams and shouting. The train descended into chaos as people suddenly started rushing towards the carriage to see what was going on.

A pale-faced woman was running in the opposite direction, away from the carriage. "There's two dead men," she yelled frantically, "In the next carriage."

David blinked. Did he hear that right? Two dead men in the carriage behind. This was something out of a film.

He peered through the carriage door to see it for himself, nervously nudging a couple of shocked passengers to the side before meeting a large crowd that had gathered at the entrance of the next carriage. David peered over their heads and looked around the carriage.

Then he saw them.

On the left, his eyes latched onto two motionless bodies. It was the two men who'd just threatened him.

Blood had run down through the seats onto the carriage floor, leaving a horrifying gory patch on the carpet. They had slumped down onto the row of seats as though they were asleep. It wasn't uncommon to see drunk people on a British train, sleeping off one too many. The men had probably been ignored by people thinking just that.

David was in shock, he wondered whether he would ever wake up from this nightmare. Although he still didn't fully believe what he was seeing, he was surprised to find that he didn't really feel any sympathy for the men.

His mind flooded with terror, how had this happened? Are there more people on the train who are following him too? Why would they have killed these two guys? This couldn't be coincidence, could it?

His anxiety was exploding, his heart racing.

The news about the dead men had spread through the carriages like a fire and it hadn't taken long for the entire train to descend into chaos. Passengers made phone calls to loved ones, journalists jumped on leads and vied to get first-hand accounts and eye-witnesses talking about the incident live on the air.

As the train pulled into Stockport, a further tremor of morbid excitement ran through the carriage as uniformed officers boarded the train moved people away from the location of the bodies and barred up the doors with blue police tape.

The crowd dispersed, rushing for the exit to leave the train as soon as possible. David left with them and walked towards the ticket barriers.

As he left the train station, he could see more police outside the station. Police cars blocking the entrances and exits to the car park. Beyond, news vans, journalists, cameramen pushed against the cordon trying to break the news first.

David started walking along Wellington Street towards Stockport city centre. He pulled out his phone and made a call to Annabel. To his relief, she answered.

"Annabel, I left the train in Stockport."

"Why would you do that? I told you to stay on until Manchester!" She began, "Is everything ok?" Her annoyance evolved into worry.

"I can try and explain it all when I see you. Can you pick me up from the Merseyway shopping centre? I'm headed there now, should be about ten minutes."

"I'll be there in half an hour."

David hung up, turned his collar up against the cold and picked up the pace.

16

Ander and Marco walked down the stairs in an awkward silence. Marco shut down Ander's clumsy attempt to break the silence with small talk about their mother.

"For once, Ander, brother – stay quiet."

Despite the decade gap in age, Marco and Ander had often been mistaken for twins. They were the same height, and both had deep, dark, murky brown eyes with dark, thick hair sat on top of slick, narrow and cleanly shaven faces, framed by sharp jawlines.

Ander had always liked to think he was in control and when they were younger, and he was right. But more recently, Marco had begun to try and detach himself from his brother. He didn't agree with some of his morals and principles and the way he went about his business, especially when Ander tried to drag him into it. The brothers shared the same hunger for success, but Marco didn't allow his morals to be compromised in order to prosper. He had built an impeccable reputation for himself in the industry, but each time Ander appeared, he feared it would come crashing down.

On the ground floor, Victoria had the desk phone to her ear. It was obvious that she was pretending to talk to someone in an effort to avoid any conversation with Ander again. She smiled sheepishly through her rigid cheeks at Marco as they walked by, though his eyes seemed to look everywhere except back at her. Once they had passed, Ander heard the clunk of the phone being placed back in its cradle.

They exited the building and started walking towards the playing fields. Marco turned towards Ander and began to talk.

"Brother, if you are going to walk into the building and try to talk football business with me or the others, do not do it in this way," he was wearing the serious face that Ander had seen many times before. Even when they were younger, his little brother would try to control him with his dominating demeanour.

"What do you mean?" Ander replied, feigning ignorance, "Obviously I have to talk about football with them and about the players I can bring to this club. How do you want me to talk to them?"

Marco was irritated, he didn't appreciate Ander's mock naivety, "You can't just come in and tell people to sign players of yours because they're Basque and that we need to support all the Basque players you have on your portfolio," he said, "This is not Athletic Bilbao. You need to understand that we don't own this club, brother, we just manage it. This is an English club owned by Americans."

He paused; his voice sounded more disappointed than angry.

"I don't want you to talk to my people like that. It is just downright rude. You are not their boss. You are not in the management. How many times have I asked you not to use me or my name to push players into or out of the club as you wish?" he brought up a finger to point at Ander, stopping his response in his throat. "Don't even think of accusing me of betraying you here either, we have signed plenty of your players in the past. Don't you see that? Why are you so stubborn on this last deal? It is one deal, why do you want it so badly?"

Ander was furious, but he couldn't reveal why this was so important to him. Other people – especially Marco – didn't appreciate the presence of The Table in international football. The truth is, even to Ander, they were a little scary. The Table was an anonymous club full of the richest people in the game, whose power stretched into all corners of the game. Their reach was so expansive that they always got what they want, and that was what Ander desired the most. Not having to toil, not having to lean on his little brother so heavily. But also, with great power came considerable wealth, and a privilege that knew no bounds. As a member of The Table, you had access to everything the world had to offer and the finances to back it up.

There was also another set of rumours. In hushed tones, people spoke of the Table as a cartel, using their money and their connections to exert pressure on people in order to get their own way.

"I've been in this world for more than twenty years, little brother. I don't need the lesson." Ander took the chance to play on his brother's emotions. "I can't believe the tone you're taking. It sounds like you've forgotten what I've done for you. The things I've sacrificed. The mornings I spent taking you to the training ground and to the games on the weekends. I bought you your football boots for God's sake, with the money I earned from my own hard work." He locked Marco in a tractor-beam gaze as he spoke. "All funded through working countless nights in the factory. Just so you could fulfil your potential on the pitch. You have forgotten who kept our lives running whilst our dad was in prison. Yet now you don't trust me, you ridicule me, and you listen to Aitor instead. He's not your blood, Marco." Ander finished triumphantly, already feeling like he'd won the argument. Once Marco might have been ashamed, reminded at what his older brother had sacrificed to help him achieve his goals, but Ander saw none of that in his face.

Marco stood firm, "Why do you bring this family shit up every time you're over here, Ander? It's growing tired. Of course, I appreciate what you have done for me." He kept his voice low, trying not to draw attention to their discussion. It irritated Ander, who'd been unable to keep a lid on his emotions as he castigated Marco.

"But I did my bit, I gave everything to make you, mum and dad proud and gave back as much as I could and then some. You've had more than your fair share of action out of this club. I have gone against my better judgement for you, signing underwhelming players. Players who weren't good enough. I did it because you are my brother, because I knew what I owed."

Marco laughed sarcastically, "Have I ever asked you for anything on that? You are far richer than me, Ander. As for trusting people here, I don't trust anyone here as far as I can throw them. But they're good at their jobs and I need them on my side in order to win. That's all I want, Ander. It's all I've ever wanted." Ander could think of nothing to say to interrupt his brother's invective.

"It's over, big brother. You need to stop trying to force players into the club that we don't want to sign. I can't do it anymore. You don't realise what a difficult position you put me in."

"I wish dad were alive to see how you talk to me. The way you paid me back for my sacrifices. I made you, Marco. You've clearly forgotten… I could break you as well. I know what was done to get you to the top."

Ander shook his head in disgust. Marco had got his first big break at Bilbao. Scouts had come to watch him and one of his teammates, the two young players had been neck and neck, though the other kid had been the nephew of one of the physios at Bilbao. From an early age, Ander had developed a strong sense of the injustice of the world – how all the hard work and talent in the world wouldn't help when set against a close connection. He had needed his brother to succeed then, not just for the financial gain, but to place the Anaia name on the map and ironically, considering what he was asking of his brother now, to break the chain of injustice that nepotism brought to the game.

There had been a small clubhouse in their area, a tiny room filled with cigar smoke where hard men lounged in plastic garden furniture, playing cards on Formica tables. Ander had never been inside before, most people averted their eyes and sped up subtly as they walked past. He had made a deal that day that would change his and his brother's lives forever. He had felt no remorse when he had seen his brother's competitor many weeks after, throwing himself around on crutches, both legs cased in plaster.

"I don't want to argue with you anymore Marco. I just need this final deal. Then I'll leave you and your club alone and will never ask you for a favour again. That's it."

Marco looked back at him puzzled.

"This deal is crucial for me," Ander continued, "Only this deal brother, you have to understand. Nothing more in the future. I promise." Marco hadn't ever seen his brother so seemingly desperate before. Ander was almost begging. He gazed at his brother, looking for a glimpse of sympathy.

Then it clicked.

"It's The Table isn't it!" Marco scoffed, "You want to join that bunch of criminals? Have you totally lost it? I know you're a hard negotiator, Ander, but those guys would do anything to protect their own interests. How can you wish to be a part of that?"

Marco paused, he didn't quite know how to vent his disappointment in his brother, "You dare question mine and Aitor's principles, but maybe you should start asking yourself. I refuse to help you become one of those crooks. You've shot yourself in the foot and given me another reason not to do this deal Ander. I think you should leave."

Marco nodded in the direction of the exit and turned to walk away. Ander grabbed his shoulder. He wasn't ready to give this up yet.

"Criminals?" Ander laughed, "Come on Marco, you of all people should know better than to believe everything you read in the papers. And anyway, you don't know what I've already given up to get us where we are."

Marco didn't know how personal his older brother was being. "Give it up Ander. I couldn't have helped you anyway, but after this nonsense about The Table, I won't even try." Marco was firm now, not giving Ander the chance to respond. "Anyway, the German lad is the exact type of player I need to complete my team. Please leave it now, let me do my work and you can do yours."

Ander took a deep breath, he looked as though he was holding something back. His brother gave him no other choice. This was Ander's last option. He felt a guilty ache in his stomach as he tried to stare a hole into the floor beneath his feet.

Marco noticed his brother's pained expression. "Understood?" he asked bluntly.

Ander's eyes flicked up to his brother, just about managing to hold his gaze, "Understood, Marco. You're damaging my business, but worse, you're damaging our family by refusing to help me. It will be the second family you've torn apart... the third, maybe. I hope you're not expecting me to help you out when a journalist calls you, armed with pictures and videos of your affair!"

Marco's jaw dropped as Ander felt an immediate rush of regret and guilt swamp through his veins.

Marco fumbled for words. Ander had caught him by surprise, "What bullshit is this now Ander?"

Ander was almost tempted to wriggle his way out of what he had just said. He took a moment to remember why he was doing this and stuck to his plan, "Did you really think your older brother wouldn't find out about your affair with Victoria?"

17

"What do you want then, Ander?"

The two brothers stood, staring each other down.

"I want my deal to get through little brother," Ander responded, trying to keep his composure. His voice wavered slightly as he spoke, "That's all. This will be the last time and then you will never be troubled by me again. I promise you. Just this one last time. You help me now and I'll make sure your affair never comes out."

There was a pause as Ander decided how to continue.

"You should be careful little brother," he emphasized, "Imagine if Maria found out. Imagine the negative press. Your kids, mum, the entire village would be asking about it. The great image you have created over the years would be completely tarnished. Everyone would feel betrayed by you." Ander was shocked at how easy he found it to press his brother. He knew exactly how to push Marco's buttons. "Forget being seen as the successful manager, the perfect family man."

Marco's face was pale, his forehead lined with sweat, "You don't know everything Ander. It's not how it seems."

Ander stooped his head to catch his brother's eye. "How do you think Maria would see it?"

Marco shook his head slowly and grunted.

"How many times have I told you?" Ander continued, showing no signs of letting off, "Don't underestimate me. I have eyes and ears everywhere. Information is key in this business. To be honest with you, I was surprised when I was told about you and Victoria, I didn't want to believe it. That's not the kind of thing we Basque people do."

Marco sighed heavily, unsure what to say, "I don't want to talk about it," he mumbled.

"Of course you don't want to!" Ander scoffed, "Who would want to talk about a two year affair that's just been found out? I have no idea how you go back home every night and look Maria and your kids in the eyes. Have you no shame? No guilt?"

Ander paused, allowing his words to sink in and have their effect upon Marco.

"You tell me not to mix up business with family. Is that not exactly what you are doing? I know that Andoni knows about it. What will his wife think too when she finds out that her husband was covering for you? His wife is friends with Maria, isn't she? Think how many relationships you would ruin. What a scandal it would be... My little brother, you are not perfect like everyone thinks. Maybe it's time that people find out about the truth. What do you think, are you really ready for that?"

Ander paused again, "Unless there was an easier option..."

Marco looked at his brother with despair, in disbelief at this cruel betrayal. But knew that he was helpless. The affair getting out would destroy so much more than his career.

"Okay," he took a deep breath, "Let's talk about the deal. The guys in the management decided they're going to sign the German instead. He should land soon, so it may not be possible to do anything about it now." Ander affected disappointment but raised his eyebrows at Marco as he pointedly took out his phone.

"Who do you think could break it fastest? Annabel at the Guardian, do you think? She'd love the injustice of it all, wouldn't she?" Ander scrolled through his contacts.

"Look, I really do want to help you but it's not as easy as you think."

Ander was satisfied his brother had finally chosen the right side, "Leave the player and his agent to me, I can deal with them. You just need to convince the rest of the management. Call the owners if necessary. They love you and would do anything you say. Tell them that if they want to sign a new deal with you, this deal needs to happen first. They must owe you a favour, no? Most do."

"You are putting me in a very difficult situation here Ander," sighed Marco.

"Well, if you could control yourself around Victoria, it wouldn't be so difficult, would it Marco?" Ander raised his hands up and shrugged. "You are the only one who can turn this around brother. I have faith in you. I know your family is more important than your business. Don't risk that. I will arrange a private jet for Markel and bring him over tonight. Let's finish this deal together."

Marco looked at the floor, nodding solemnly, "This is the last time I am doing a deal with you Ander. If you mention the Victoria issue again, we will never see each other for as long as I live. Already I know I will struggle to ever forgive you for this blackmail. You talk of the pride of the Basque people. A Basque would never do this. A brother wouldn't."

"Don't worry, little bro," Ander smiled, placing a reassuring hand on Marco's shoulder, "I will take it to the grave with me, but you should really start being more careful. Remember who you are and the responsibility your job carries. I had to pay millions to stop the pictures leaking. You owe me for that, and it won't get any cheaper if it carries on. I know you are angry right now, but you will thank me one day. Think about that before blaming me for your sins."

"I understand." Marco said, resigned.

"I hope you do."

As Ander left the training complex, he realized he still hadn't heard from Joska. He figured she was probably at the beach like she'd said. The latest fight with her mother looked like it had really taken something out of her. She needed some time to be alone.

He opened up the message.

SOS need help urgently

His heart skipped a beat. What had happened? She had only been alone for a few hours. Was she hurt? He began typing out a text, but half-way through thought it was best to call. The line went straight through to voicemail.

"Joska, it's dad. I just got your message. Call me back."

He tried to console himself, but he couldn't stop thinking about Joska's message. Was it accidental? Had she accidentally sent the message, perhaps sitting on her phone? If that was the case, then why was her phone switched off now. If he knew his daughter, it was social suicide for her phone to be dead. No, he thought, if there was a real emergency, Joska would have called again.

His phone vibrated in his breast pocket and his heart stopped racing. Number withheld. Could this be her? If her phone had died, then maybe she was using another to get in touch with him. He connected the call.

"Joska, are you okay? I just left a message, only just saw your text."

"Mr. Anaia, so nice to finally be in touch." It was not Joska. He had been expecting this call.

"It's been quite a long day," Ander fought down his nerves about his daughter and adopted his most serious, business-like tone. He was trying to impress whoever was on the other line.

"So I hear. And you're not the only one. I hope the deal is coming along nicely. There's a lot resting on this, as you know – and not just for you and your player."

Ander's confidence was at its peak as he replied. "Everything is proceeding exactly as planned. There was a brief misunderstanding this morning, but—"

"A misunderstanding? Interesting. Well, we wouldn't want there to be any lack of clarit—"

"No, no, nothing to worry about it's all ironed out now."

"Mr. Anaia, please have the decency to never interrupt me again. I want to make it perfectly clear that your acceptance to this esteemed club relies entirely on your making this deal happen today. There is no margin for error."

Ander's confidence had taken a blow. He felt as though he were being reprimanded by an old headmaster.

"I know, believe me. As I was saying, it was just a small misunderstanding. A slight realignment of the sporting director and a stern word with my brother, but it's all running smoothly now."

"Good. I believe you're trying your hardest, I really do. I just wanted to share something with you, something that might give you that extra bit of push. Switch to video."

Ander thought this was very strange, but he was excited at the prospect of finally seeing the face of the man he'd been speaking to for months now.

He held his phone up, subtly affecting the angle so the camera caught him in a good light.

What he saw next completely broke him. The image on the screen was dark, murky, but he could see her as clear as day. Joska, huddled in the corner of a dank room, lit only by a bare overhead bulb. Her knees were pulled up tight to her chest. The feed looked like it was being taken from a security camera. As it zoomed in on Joska, her eyes darted towards the camera, alerted by the noise.

Ander's stomach dropped out of him.

"What the fuck is this? Is this some kind of joke?" he could barely contain his… his what? His rage? His fear? He forced himself to control the myriad emotions racing through him at that moment.

"I can ensure you, Mr. Anaia, it is no joke," the other man seemed to be enjoying Ander's pain. "Joska is fine and will continue to be fine as long as you uphold your end of the bargain. You might consider it insurance, I suppose."

"Let me speak to her," Ander's voice was raised.

"Mr. Anaia. Ander. You are in absolutely no position to make such demands. You need to trust me. Your daughter is fine, and no harm will come to her, providing your player signs with Manchester United tomorrow afternoon."

Ander's stomach lurched. He looked again at the grainy image. He could just about make out the details of Joska's face. She had been crying, her eyes were puffy. But she didn't look hurt. It didn't look like they'd been physical with her, and he could see a tray full of half-eaten food.

They were trying to power trip him, letting him know the sort of power he was dealing with. The sort of power that he'd have access to if this deal went off and he took his rightful seat at The Table. He took a moment to consider that. Was this the sort of power he wanted? Was it worth it?

"Just make sure she comes back to me unharmed," Ander decided to push back hard, "If I find a single mark on my daughter, I will find the man responsible and have him punished. Severely."

"Well," the man on the other end of the line sounded impressed, "Looks like this cat has claws. Goodbye, Mr. Anaia. I hope that the next time we speak will be on more positive terms. And needless to say, let's keep this between us. We don't need the authorities breathing down our necks and I know you feel the same way." With that, he disconnected the call.

Ander pocketed his phone and took a deep breath. He needed to get this deal done, fast.

18

"Hello?" Joska called out to her guard. "I need to empty this bucket, please. Unless you want to do it?" She had made the decision that she needed to get out of this place. She didn't know what her dad was into, but she'd seen enough movies to know that the sooner she could get out of here the better. Who knew if they'd make good on their promise to let her go?

She heard the sound of the man raising up from his chair, the jangle of keys, the metal clunk of the bolt turning in the door. The door opened part of the way, the light from the hall brightening up the squalor of Joska's cell.

"Come," the man said, and Joska opened the door all the way. She had been in the dark for hours, now, and the bright overhead incandescent lights smarted her eyes. She raised a hand to shield them as she trod carefully out into the hallway.

The stark white corridor stretched out both ways for several meters, with a door at either end. Through high windows, she saw feet walking past, though she couldn't hear the footsteps, which suggested thick, impenetrable security glass. It would make screaming for help a complete waste of time.

“That way,” the man placed his hand on her shoulder and guided her left, down the hall. She pushed through the door at the end and walked straight into a tiny closet bathroom with barely enough room to fit a toilet and sink. It reminded Joska of her favourite restaurant by the coast near her dad’s house. A tiny ramshackle place, family run for generations. They served the most beautiful traditional Basque food, which you could see them cooking in the back of the restaurant. The bathroom always seemed to be down a tiny, steep staircase next to the kitchen, and you had to navigate old, empty tins of cooking oil and spare paper towels to get there.

The guard kept his foot wedged in the door the whole time she was in the room, though for what reason, Joska couldn’t fathom. The room was essentially a closet with at toilet in it – it wasn’t like she could stage an escape through the U-Bend.

She tipped away the contents of the bucket and washed her hands in the tiny basin.

“Don’t push your luck, girl,” He hurried her along. You’re not that cute. Back to your room.” Joska could feel his eyes on her.

“Sorry, sir,” she replied, placing her hand on his chest, squeezing slightly.

He stepped back swiftly, unmoved by her advances, and allowed her to pass. He fell into step behind her as she made her way back to the door. She took a step inside, but as he grabbed the handle to close it, she turned, using her body to block the gap in the door.

"Hey, don't go," she said, and saw his eyebrows raise almost imperceptibly. A smile crept from his mouth to his eyes. "Could I have another blanket?"

His eyes narrowed slightly as he tried to read her. "Let me see what I can find."

He returned quickly with a ratty cotton throw, his small smile had broadened into a grin. He reached the throw out to her, snatching it back as she reached out to take it. She edged forward, gripping the blanket, and pulled it towards her. He moved with her as she pulled the blanket and then they were both suddenly inside her cell.

"It gets pretty cold in here," she had dropped the Basque now, fallen back to Spanish. She moved her hand to his and moved them further into the room.

The man let go of the blanket and made to kiss her on the mouth. She moved her head to one side, offering him her neck and shoved his face against her, his day-old stubble scratching against her. As his hands moved to her waist, Joska tightened her grip on the cotton throw she had in one hand, pulling it taught with her other hand as the guard lost himself, placing kisses along her collarbone. She groaned in mock appreciation and then in one swift movement moved round to his back, bringing the blanket up to his throat.

She raised one leg up, her knee pressing into the man's back as she twisted the blanket around itself, corkscrewing it tight. The years of self-defence training that she'd hoped to never have to use were coming into their own now. The man's hands clutched at the fabric, but he was unable to get any purchase. As the oxygen began to cut off, Joska felt him getting weaker and he eventually dropped to his knees. She put her foot up to his back now, pulling back with her whole weight. He continued to grasp at the fabric, but his grip was slack, his hands padding uselessly at the livid purple of his neck.

As his hands slumped to his sides, Joska released her grip on the blanket and rolled the man into the corner. He was a dead weight and she had to use all of her strength to move him just a short distance. She checked for a pulse, found one, then began undressing him. She put on his t-shirt and bundled up the rest of his clothes and underwear, tucking it under her arm. She picked up the keys that he had dropped during the struggle and locked the door behind her as she made her way out into the hall.

19

The Merseyway shopping centre had been built more than fifty years ago over the River Mersey. It had two levels, connected by escalators, providing access to almost one hundred shops. It was one of the first shopping centres of its kind in the United Kingdom.

The building itself was overwhelming. All around David bright lights and vibrant signs shone back at him. The walkways seemed to be never-ending as the streaks of shops and restaurants lined up next to each other.

David had entered the through the grand glass entrance and looked for a place to get a coffee before Annabel arrived.

He stood looking up at the menu in Costa, his face scrunched up in disapproval as he ordered a cappuccino with almond milk.

He couldn't take his mind off of what had happened on the train. He had so many questions. Who exactly were the two men on the train? And who killed them and why? Did they get killed because they were following and threatening me? It seemed too much of a coincidence that the same two men who had threatened him would wind up dead moments later. He had seen the bodies, seen the execution style wounds. These were not messy kills, the work of a professional.

His thoughts returned to his father. He needed to try calling again. A lump formed in his throat when there was still no answer. He began to invent scenarios where men like those he'd met forced their way into his family home. His dad was getting on a bit now, but there was no way he'd take a home invasion lying down.

He winced as he took a sip of his coffee and called again. A great wave of relief washed over him when the call connected.

"Hello, son," A grin spread across David's face at the sound of his father's voice, "How are you? Big day today, eh? How's it going?"

David didn't even think about telling his dad what had just happened, he was just glad to hear from him.

"I'm good, dad. I was worried because I haven't been able to reach you all morning."

"Oh, sorry David, we had some issues with electricity in the house and I couldn't charge my phone." David could hear the phony nonchalance in his dad's voice. Had the electricity been cut off in their house? Had they missed their bills? He decided to ignore it for now, he'd talk to him about it when things were a little more settled. Once the deal was done and he could offer him some real money to sort everything out.

"Well anyway, I'm glad that everything is fine. How is gran?"

"She's good. Misses you a lot. You should visit us soon."

"I'll be there soon, dad. I'll come up after I'm done in Manchester. I've missed you both."

"Brilliant," his dad replied, David could feel him smiling down the phone, "Look, I have to shoot off – Gran's got an appointment in town and I'm driving her down. Take care of yourself, son."

David tried to tell his dad that he loved him, but he had already rung off.

He felt a huge sense of relief. His family was fine. One less thing to worry about.

He scrolled through his phone and called the boys in the office.

"Hi David, are you in Manchester already?" asked Jose.

"Not quite. I got off the train early. I'll explain later. How are you guys getting on with the contracts so far? Anything unusual? Put me on speaker."

"Hi David," William shouted over from his desk, "all good over here. We've just had lunch and then come back to the office to crack on. Nothing unusual in the contract as far as we can see. Have you received Schedule Two yet?"

"I'm glad you guys are okay," the more he heard the calm in William and Jose, the more David began to feel less on edge about the whole situation. He'd been spooked by the guys on the train, but maybe they were just idle threats, trying to throw him off the deal. Maybe their deaths were coincidence after all. It wouldn't be too much of a stretch to imagine that guys like that also had people after them from time to time. "Still nothing, I just checked my inbox. I'll try to get through to Aitor."

"Remember he's Basque," said William, "It's the afternoon; he might be having his siesta right now." David laughed.

"Has Patrick arrived in Manchester?" asked Jose, rolling his eyes at William.

"He's just about to land. The club will drop him at the hotel."

"Sounds good David. We're here for the rest of the day, let us know if there is anything you need. I'll buy the cigars later as well," said Jose, his tone buoyant.

David chuckled, "Get Cohibas!"

"Of course, amigo. Only the best."

"Talk to you both later, lads. Take it easy. And please, keep your eyes on a swivel when you're out and about. Those guys on the train were very sketchy. They knew a lot about us…" David said cautiously.

"Don't worry about us, David. But yes, we'll keep them peeled."

David hung up as he took the escalator to the second floor. His phone was running out of battery, but he needed to call Aitor.

He dialled the number and rang, taking a deep breath. This was an important call.

"David!" Aitor spoke in a friendly Basque accent, "How are you, my friend?"

"Good afternoon, Aitor. I'm well, thanks. Just on my way up to Manchester now."

"Good to hear. Is Patrick here already? Or arriving soon at least? I need to send the driver to the airport so just let me know when he gets in. Looking forward to seeing you both first thing tomorrow. Let me know if you need anything else in the meantime. I have arranged two rooms at the Edwardian Radisson Blu for you both. You are our guest obviously; it's all on us!" Aitor was clearly on the full charm offensive.

David couldn't help but be impressed at it all. "Thanks for arranging the driver and for the hotel rooms. That wasn't necessary, appreciate that."

"That's the least we can do David," to his credit, Aitor sounded genuinely excited, "Can I do anything else for you?"

"Actually, yes Aitor." David felt bad having to bring up business when he'd just been given the star treatment. "I still haven't received Schedule Two of the contract. I would like to be able to go through it with Patrick in the hotel this evening. I've told him all the figures but it would be nice to get it in front of him so he can see it and exactly what he is signing tomorrow," said David, trying to sound as confident as possible.

"Oh, I'm so sorry my friend. I thought it had already been sent with the other documents we sent over last week. I'll get my assistant to do it." Aitor apologized, but David didn't fully believe him. He wasn't sure what sort of mind game Aitor was playing, but at least it was sorted now so it was best to stay polite.

"No worries at all, Aitor. These things happen and I didn't want to bother you. I know how busy you guys must be right now. It doesn't get busier than the end of the transfer window!"

"Thanks for your understanding, David," Aitor said sincerely, "I'll talk to you, at the latest tomorrow morning, but feel free to give me a ring if you need anything else." They made their goodbyes and David hung up the call.

He wasn't convinced by Aitor's performance. He was definitely lying about the missing Schedule Two just being an oversight. David had emailed him as soon as he saw it was missing and Aitor had never answered. He hadn't once picked up the phone when David had rung before. Never responded to any messages. Not until Aitor's scouting department had picked up on Patrick as their first target. He had completely ignored David, until David had something that Aitor needed. Now he was calling him his friend. They were all the same, these people. Snakes in the grass. He loved his job so much. Loved the game. But so far, he'd not loved many people he'd met in the industry. Far from it.

David had finished his coffee and was making his way downstairs when a pair of hands covered his eyes. He started and span wildly, throwing himself away from his attacker.

"Whoa, whoa! Easy tiger," said a female voice, as she unclasped her hands, raising them in front of her, showing she was no threat.

"Annabel!" exclaimed David, struggling to hide his childish grin.

He had been looking forward to seeing her, in fact, he was always excited to see her.

"Are we just going to ignore that?" she said, waving her hand in his general direction.

"Sorry, it's been a very weird day." David realised how strange his reaction must have seemed.

"You can tell me all about it. It's great to see you again, it's been far too long. You look good," Annabel said, reaching out to take his hand. "Come on, I'm parked outside." And with that, she led him down the escalator and towards the rear of the shopping centre where the car park was.

Annabel was a small, pretty young woman in her late twenties with long dark hair with dyed blonde streaks, and eyes that David could get lost in for days. Her smile could light up a room and her vibrant, bubbly personality was impossible not to love. But she was also fierce. In just a few short years, she had established herself as a formidable force in the world of investigative sports journalism.

David had met Annabel after he'd graduated and moved to London. He had been sending off some job applications from the comfort of 39 Steps Coffee and Annabel happened to be working there, covering some of her expenses by working a part time job alongside her study. He had been instantly entranced by her and became a regular customer at the coffee shop. He'd actually worked out which shifts she usually worked, and he'd make sure he was there to see her. It made him feel like a stalker, but she had laughed when he mentioned it, and they had grown very close as friends.

David had never plucked up the courage to take it to the next level. He was sure that his feelings were reciprocated, but the thought that they might not be, and that mentioning it would destroy the friendship that they had, always stopped him from doing anything.

Annabel had moved north to pursue an opportunity with the BBC in Manchester where her career had blossomed, leaving David behind in London. She had quickly risen through the ranks and was already one of their leading investigators.

Part of the attraction of working with Manchester United was that he'd be able to see Annabel when he went up there. He clung onto the hope that one day they would become something more.

For now, though, their focus was on the business at hand.

"There's a lot we need to go over," she turned towards David as they took the elevator to her car. "I've got a story that I've been building for a while now about nepotism in the industry. The Anaia's are the perfect route in. But we need to wait for the right time to break it. I don't want to kill your de—"

"Annabel," he stopped her, "I need to tell you something important; the reason why I got off here."

She looked at him anxiously.

"I was approached by two people that I'd seen earlier this morning in London. They were on the train with me and threatened me during the journey, telling me to get off before Manchester. I wasn't sure what to do but before I could decide… well, everything turned to chaos. I'm sure you've seen the news reports by now. Those two dead guys they found on the train were the same one who threatened me. I can't decide whether it's just a really morbid coincidence, or we're in a lot deeper trouble than either of us realise." This was the first time David had spoken to anyone about the incident, and he felt the words pouring out of him. He barely drew breath as he unloaded onto her. It felt good, but he could feel his emotions rising the more he spoke.

Annabel cast her eyes around the crowds in the shopping mall, "It's probably best to talk about this somewhere else. My car is just here. As I say, there's a lot to go over."

She tightened her grip on his hand as she pulled him out of the elevator into the multi-story parking lot.

Despite the situation, a fuzzy feeling rushed through David. His heart was thumping. He forgot everything that was happening in the world and was entranced by the grip of her hand around his. She started talking about something, he registered none of it.

"David?" She shook his arm, almost shouting, "did you hear me? Are you ok?"

"Yes, sorry" spluttered David, slightly embarrassed, "I'm just still in shock," he lied, still trying to enjoy the moment.

Annabel pointed over to a poorly lit space in the corner, "There we are. That's my car."

It was a black Mercedes Viano. As they got closer David noticed it had blacked out glass in the windows.

"You love your privacy don't you," David joked, whilst climbing into the back seat.

Annabel didn't pick up on David's attempt to flirt, "Yes I do. I have a lot of meetings in my car. So, I need to have some privacy," she responded. "Don't need the hacks spying on who I'm meeting. And now we're trying to break this nepotism and corruption thing with the rogue agents, it's even more important. Whistle-blowers like to remain hidden."

"Back to my office, please," said Annabel.

Only now did David notice the bearded middle-aged driver in the front of the car. He had been too fixated upon Annabel to notice anyone else.

The man said nothing, and the car pulled silently out of the parking lot and out into the city outside. He raised the window separating the back from the front of the car, and placed earphones in.

David asked Annabel about the man.

"Oh, don't mind Malik. I'd trust him with my life. He's been on my team since day one." Annabel reassured David.

"If you trust him, then what's with the soundproof glass?" asked David.

"The less he knows, the easier it is for him. And the more I can trust him."

Malik pulled away from the exit of the car park and set off towards the signs to Manchester.

20

Marco slumped into the chair in his office, contemplating his options. Over the years, his brother had put him in a several difficult situations, but this time he had overstepped the mark.

Marco was furious, shocked that his brother would threaten him with such a thing as the affair. He found little consolation in Ander protecting him by paying the journalist, he'd only done it so that he could use it against Marco himself.

How could he?

Marco sat with his head in his hands, his palms sweaty and his leg twitching nervously under the desk.

It was true that Ander had done a lot in the past for Marco and their mother, especially when their dad had been in prison. Marco had respected this and helped Ander with countless deals over the years, making him plenty of money. But there came a point where it had to stop, where that debt was paid.

Ander opened the door and calmly strolled into the office. He took a seat opposite his brother, blew on his mug to cool the coffee down and looked at Marco. Ander looked like he meant business.

"I see you helped yourself to coffee," Marco said.

Ander ignored his sarcasm. "By the way," he began, "If you don't sign him, I will not renew the contracts of my other two talents. Tell the management they can forget about the contract offers they gave to me two weeks ago.

Did you see them in the under twenty-ones? One got the golden boot; the other was player of the tournament. I have better options for them in the Premier League. Financially, they could be far better off than what they earn here. The renewal offers are far below the sums of money they would be able to get elsewhere.

Nonetheless, I was going to convince them to sign the dotted line and renew with you guys. I was going to do it to help you, Marco," Ander paused to sip his coffee, searching for some appreciation in his brother's face. Marco gazed blankly back over the desk.

He shook his head, "The boys want to stay here Ander, you know that..."

"The boys just want the best for their career," Ander interrupted, "I have looked after them since they were fifteen. They would never sign anything without my approval," Ander oozing superiority, "Everything I have ever advised them to do has benefitted them, they listen to me, respect me and will do as I tell them. I employ both of their fathers as scouts, arranged scholarships for their brothers and sisters, built houses for their mothers. Do you really think these boys and their families will not listen to me?"

Marco was on the back foot, "The contracts we have offered them are huge, Ander. They may well get better elsewhere but they want to play for United and we are prepared to pay them more than enough to be able to look after their own families now."

"That's not how they work Marco. Do you really want to test their loyalties?" Ander asked rhetorically, "Besides, it's not just their careers they owe me for. They both found themselves in very similar circumstances to you, brother. They had some very interesting parties, filled with pretty British girls and, unfortunately, a cameraman on one occasion."

"And let me guess," Marco interrupted begrudgingly, "The journalist who had the video footage called you?"

Ander laughed, "Of course he did, brother. He understands the business we are in. He gets his bonus and I take the footage to protect it and then we move on."

Ander took another sip from his coffee as his brother looked towards the floor, "For the time being, anyway."

Marco refocused, peering pensively at his brother, "For the time being?" he asked.

"Come on, Marco. We both know you can't rely on the goodness of other people's hearts. Loyalty is a tightrope. I need to protect myself." Ander laughed through his nose.

"Let me ask you something Ander. Have you ever used something like that?" Marco asked, unsure if he wanted to hear the answer.

Ander grinned like a Hollywood villain, "What do you think brother?"

With that, he stood from his chair and walked out the office, still clutching his coffee.

"Let me know any updates when you hear them, brother," he emphasized the last word like a full stop, turned and let himself out of the room.

Marco leaned back, staring up at the ceiling, his mind whirring.

As he became lost in his own thought, he was abruptly jolted back to reality as Andoni burst into his room.

"Are you talking to yourself, amigo?" said Andoni.

"Oh, Andoni," Marco huffed, realizing that he'd been muttering to himself, "I don't even know where to start."

He had always kept an open and close relationship with Andoni. Andoni had been the CEO at United for five years and had done an almost exemplary job, except from the hiring of his brother-in-law, Aitor, but you could forgive him for wanting to keep his sister happy.

Andoni's huge frame seemed to occupy a room no matter how large, but he was as gentle as a giant could come. Despite his friendly and approachable nature, he was also a brilliant businessman and negotiator. His warm smile, infectious laugh and clockwork brain could bring almost any opponent to their knees.

Most importantly for Marco, he was tolerant and understanding, particularly with Ander. Marco had always felt he could trust Andoni with anything, and regularly confided in him. Andoni was the first to know about Marco's affair, and Marco was confident he would keep it confidential, though he had been very disappointed to hear the news. Andoni was a family man and believed in the sanctity of marriage vows.

Andoni shook his head, tutting, "I know, Marco. I sympathise with you. It's the same with Ander every time, isn't it?"

"You're right, it happens every year but it's more difficult this time, my friend," Marco responded gravely.

Andoni looked puzzled, raising his left eyebrow, "What do you mean more difficult? He is just trying to push his player from Bilbao into the club. We won't let it happen, not this time Marco. You promised me you wouldn't support him anymore if he offered us a player we don't want."

Marco had hoped Andoni would let it slide. "Yes, I did," he admitted, "But it's complicated, Andoni."

"Look Marco, we discussed this with the owners in Los Angeles. They have to deal with all the complaints about your brother and his dealings here. The truth is, no one wants him around," Andoni said cautiously, trying not to cause Marco too much offence, he knew that family and Ander were important to him. To his surprise, Marco nodded in agreement, "Even the security guys complain about the way he treats them. He has far too much influence in every single department in this club. He is watching us, listening to us, controlling us. The owners were clear. We will not sign a player if they are not approved by the scouts, by Aitor, and you and me together. It's a decision we take as a collective from now on. The decision has been made already. We had three left wingers on the list and our number one target is the German boy. He will land in Manchester imminently. Your brother's player is number three. That's the suggestion we gave to the board, and they have confirmed it."

Marco looked worried and Andoni felt for him, he knew the difficult positions his brother had put him in over the years, but he also knew that he had to make his point. "Everyone knows the culture is changing in our club, Marco. We need to be more professional, my friend. This is not a family business, and we don't own this place. We all have our own responsibilities, and we are accountable for our actions."

Marco was visibly distressed, "I agree with everything you say my friend and you have always backed me. Even during the times when I supported my brother with a deal that wasn't right for us. I owe you a lot."

Andoni chuckled, "You do owe me, amigo. Ander's never caused problems between us, but his power has to be stopped at some point."

Marco looked at the floor, "This time it's about Maria," he said shamefully.

"About Maria?" Andoni said, surprised, "I don't understand. What does she have to do with anything?"

Marco looked on the brink of tears, "Ander threatened me, he knows about my affair with Victoria, and he has video footage. He even silenced a journalist so he could use it himself."

Andoni stared at Marco's forlorn figure silently. He turned and walked over to the cabinet on the far side of the room. He pulled out a cut crystal glass and poured himself a generous glass of whisky. He ran his hand over a wooden box on the side, lifted the lid and took out a Cohiba. Cutting off the tip he lit a match and rolled the cigar in his fingers, warming the tip and drawing long and slow, the tobacco leaf catching. He took a big draw, the cherry glowing orange, and let out a long plume of smoke. They usually reserved these to be smoked after a great victory. Today felt more like a defeat. A terrible defeat.

21

Joska worked her way down another long corridor. Each one she'd found so far was almost identical. Peeling white paint and plain concrete floors, discoloured at the edges there was a light path worn through the grime that seemed almost to light her way.

One corridor led to another until she came across a heavy fire door. She slammed her hands into the sprung bar that lay across it and emerged into a stairwell.

The bare concrete block walls rose up several floors, the staircase coiling around the edge. Joska could see right to the ceiling through the gap in the spiral.

Joska set off up the stairs until she reached the first floor. She peered through the porthole in the door and found a dimly lit room, mahogany and leather covering the walls. Vintage Scandinavian furniture was artfully scattered throughout, amongst wingback armchairs and low coffee tables adorned with magazines. It looked like the lounge in a high-end hotel or a private members club. Realising she must be at street level she felt for a door handle but realised there was none.

She turned and headed up another set of stairs. It was four flights until she found a door with a handle. She checked through the porthole before gently opening the door and stepping through into another bare corridor, though this one had several doors leading off of it. Joska checked the signs on door. Housekeeping. Janitor. So, this is a hotel, she thought as she made her way down the corridor slowly, treading carefully on her bare feet.

She checked a few of the doors as she moved along, eventually finding one that was open. She saw a closet full of uniforms and quickly scanned through looking for something that looked like it might fit.

Pulling on overalls, she rolled up the ankles and cuffs and headed towards the small service elevator at the far end and pressed the button.

The wait was excruciating, all the time Joska prayed that it would be empty. A gentle bell announced the lift's arrival and Joska held her breath as the doors opened.

Empty.

She entered the elevator and looked at the control panel. She pressed the button for the ground floor. It wasn't until the doors closed behind her that she realised she was still holding her breath.

It seemed to take a lifetime for the elevator to start moving. Joska watched the lights on the floor indicator work their way down. Five floors. If it was a hotel she was in, it can't have been very big. Judging by the entrance lobby, it looked incredibly exclusive. Joska tried to think where they could have taken her, up in the mountains, which would warrant such luxury. All she knew of the towns in the mountains were a few places the monks had set up. It wasn't exactly an obvious destination for the wealthy elite.

The elevator stopped and Joska's head darted up. There were still three floors to go. Shit. As the doors cracked open, Joska pressed herself into the side of the elevator. Angling her head around the corner, she saw a woman dumping towels into a bin in the bottom of her chambermaid trolley. The woman wore a black tunic with a starched white penny collar and sleeve hem. There was a suggestion, Joska thought, of one of those fancy dress maid outfits, but a lot classier. It was clearly tailored and fit the woman perfectly.

Joska spotted a lanyard on top of the trolley and without hesitation she moved through the door and headed straight for it.

Before the maid had a chance to say anything, Joska had snatched up her lanyard and was halfway down the corridor. She barged through into the guest staircase and tore down the stairs looking for a place to hide. Surely the maid would alert the front desk straight away, there'd be no chance for Joska to get out that way. The woman might not know that her employers were in the business of kidnapping, but Joska could risk it. Not right now. She needed to lay low for a while.

She went through the door to the next floor. She pulled on a pair of sneakers someone had left outside their door, wincing as they pinched her toes. It was better than her bare feet, though: especially if she was planning on making it outside.

Joska didn't dare risk entering one of the rooms, though she imagined her key card opened every door in the building. She'd already got one witness alerted to her presence, she didn't need to leave more of a trail for the people who would eventually be trying to find her. When they realised she was missing.

The last door in the corridor was marked CONFERENCE SUITE 1 and Joska felt a small glimmer of hope as she swiped the key card through the reader on the door.

As she closed the door, Joska pressed her eye to the peephole and scanned the corridor she'd just left. There was no movement. Joska felt her body relax and she concentrated on bringing her breathing under control as she kept watch on the hall.

Satisfied, she turned and walked further into the space behind her. Armchairs in varying shades and textile lined the walls, on which collections of books were artfully arranged. It was definitely some boutique hotel, thought Joska. The room felt like a waiting room or airport lounge, comfortable, but practical. There was nowhere for Joska to hide away here. A single heavy oak door sat in the centre of the back wall. There was no key card reader on this door, but Joska marvelled at the ornate brass door handle.

The handle itself was shaped like a snake; its body coiled around to provide something to grip. Each scale was intricately marked out, its eyes were inset jewels.

Joska reached out and turned the handle, pushing through the door. The light in the room came from the well-fed fireplace and a few antique oil lamps on the walls. A heavy cloud of cigar smoke hung heavy in the air and Joska was briefly reminded of her dad's filthy habit. It felt like a strange reversal of roles for a kid to be telling their parent that smoking didn't make them look cool.

It took Joska a few moments to adjust to the dark. To realise that she wasn't alone.

"My dear," a voice, slick like oil, emerged from the gloom, "So nice of you to join us. Now, how did you get out?"

Joska's eyes widened as she took in the scene before her. Half a dozen men in varying stages of undress were situated around the room as groups of women performed various acts on them. She turned immediately and grabbed for the handle, ready to bolt once more, but a meaty fist grabbed her wrist and deftly brought her arm behind her back. Pain glanced through her forearm and down her spine and Joska found herself unable to break the hold. No one seemed to bat an eyelid, carrying on their tawdry antics.

In addition to the depravity, others were situated around every imaginable kind of gambling vice. Groups of men huddled around blackjack tables, roulette boards, nursing tumblers full of spirits, cigars perched on ashtrays as they threw down chips and cards.

The guard forced her over towards an impeccably turned-out man, dressed head to toe in Savile Row, who was beckoning with one hand, a tumbler of whisky in the other.

He brushed off the woman who had been sat on his lap and stood up as Joska approached.

"I'm afraid this puts us in something of an awkward situation," he said. "If you'd just done as you were asked, then assuming your father carried his end of the bargain, there would be nothing to worry about. You'd have been free to go." He took a long, laboured draw on a cigar, the cherry glowing in the gloom.

"But now you've seen us, you've seen our faces, it's not quite so simple…" he gave a brief nod and the man holding Joska subtly twisted her arm. The pain was excruciating, the only way to relieve it was to drop to her knees. As she did so, she saw her chance. She thrust her head back as hard as she could, connecting with the man's groin.

He doubled in agony, sucking in breath, and released his grip. Joska jumped up and turned, bolting for the door she'd come through. She tore at the handle, back out into the waiting room, ignoring the yelling from behind her, and burst through the hall and out into the guest staircase. She streamed down the stairs, taking two, three at a time until she finally reached the lobby she'd seen before.

A lone member of staff manned the reception desk. He looked up at the wild woman who'd just burst through into the masculine serenity of the leather-clad room, and it took him several moments to gain the presence of mind to pick up the phone.

Joska only had one choice.

She ran straight through the open doorway, through the car park, out across lush green lawns and into the wild of the tree line beyond.

22

"We're picking up Julia, on the way," said Annabel, breaking the silence that had descended in the back of the car. "We've worked together for the last four years. You can trust her like you trust me. No one knows that she works for me. There is a meeting point we have around Stockport, at Heaton Norris Park, she gives me all the information there."

"You work with someone?" David said surprised, "That doesn't sound like you at all." Though he had no right to be jealous, a small part of David was glad it wasn't a man who was helping Annabel.

"I know, but Julia was recommended to me by my uncle in Italy, so I gave it a try. Ever since then we've worked together. To be honest I can't complain. She's done a good job so far. How are the boys back in London?"

"They are doing well. They always ask about you. They call you my 'mysterious friend'," said David smiling.

"Well, I'll meet them eventually, I suppose," she smiled back.

"Annabel?" Malik had wound down the glass separating the back of the car from the front.

"Yes, Malik?"

"Sorry to interrupt, it's just that… not to sound too much like a Hollywood movie, but I think we're being followed. A few cars back, blacked out SUV. I've been trying to give them the slip, but they're stuck to us like flies to shit."

Annabel's brow creased as she turned to look out the rear windscreen. Sure enough, travelling two cars behind them a jet-black SUV aped every turn Malik made.

"Keep trying to lose them, Malik – I'll text Julia and let her know the change of plan."

Annabel pulled out her mobile and shot off a quick text before pocketing the device again.

"Okay," she turned back to David, "So tell me more about these dead guys on the train."

David recalled how even before the two men had approached him on the train, they'd tried to accost him in the park outside work.

"I managed to get away from them that time, but I had nowhere to go on the train. It feels bad to say it, but luckily someone else dealt with them for me," David tried to make light of the situation, but Annabel didn't see the funny side. "They were pretty nasty looking blokes. I can't imagine they made many friends. But who were they working for? And who would want them dead?"

"I think we both know this sounds like classic Ander, David," Annabel's didn't miss a beat. "I've never had the displeasure of meeting him, but I've heard so many things from people at United about how he treats everyone. I wouldn't put it past him at all to send people to scare you off the deal. I found out from one of their scouts that his player is bottom of the pile to sign."

"The question is," David said, "Are there more? Clearly whoever's following us now is working with the guys from the train."

"Don't worry about it, David – he's an arsehole, but I can't believe he'd ever go so far as to actually hurt anyone. He's just trying to scare you." Annabel knocked on the glass.

"Annabel?" Malik was keeping his eyes on his mirrors, driving steadily so as not to alert the people following them that they'd caught wind.

"Let's try and lose these blokes and get us to David's hotel. They won't try anything there – too public." Annabel turned to David, "He's good at this. Won't tell me where he learned it, but I don't really care at the end of the day – as long as he keeps me safe!"

With that, the car turned a sharp right and picked up speed along a residential street. David kept his head swivelled round, watching as the other car stopped, signalled to turn and then followed after them.

The car gently accelerated, and Malik made several more quick manoeuvres, taking side streets and bobbing and weaving the car through traffic. Finally, he swung the car left up a one-way street. The car following hadn't anticipated the move and sped right past them.

"Hold tight guys," Malik said, hitting the gas.

The car lurched forward, its powerful engine impelling them down the narrow road. David turned to Annabel, shocked and she let out a small laugh.

"Honestly, relax. We've been in a lot stickier situations than this." As she spoke, her head lurched forward as Malik slammed on the brakes and shifted the car into reverse. They sped along to the end of the road — travelling the right way now, but with the car the wrong way around – and seemingly without looking, Malik deftly spun the car back in the direction they'd come.

"Think we lost them," Malik said, a small grin spreading across his face.

"I never had any doubt in my heart, Malik," Annabel said, "Now, shall we get you to your room, David?"

23

David had made his way back down to the hotel bar from his room. Annabel was waiting for him, nursing a G&T.

"I charged it to the room – hope you don't mind? I figured United were paying..." Annabel wore a smirk. David couldn't help but smile back.

"Good point," he said, "I might as well join you then, hadn't I?" He called over a waiter and ordered an old fashioned.

"It's been quite the day already," he said, when it arrived. He wasn't accustomed to drinking in the daytime, but it felt like if now wasn't a good time, he didn't know when was.

"Too right," said Annabel, and clinked her glass against his. "Cheers... Right, so anyway, enough with all that, let's talk about the deal. What's the latest?"

"Nothing since I left the train. Patrick must have landed and will be on his way here. Obviously, I'm not going to tell him about any of this. All he needs to see is the beautiful gliding swan, not the legs kicking furiously underneath."

David took a sip of his drink and felt instantly relaxed as the warmth of the whisky hit his tastebuds. Annabel looked over his shoulder and smiled, giving a little wave.

David turned to see a woman walking across the lobby to the hotel bar. She looked to be a similar age to Annabel, and at little more than five feet tall, was about the same height. She wore glasses over her bright turquoise eyes and smiled mischievously in a slightly unsettling way.

Before Annabel could begin to introduce her, Julia had reached her hand out towards David with a big smile on her face.

"So, this is the super-agent, is it?" she said, vigorously shaking his hand casting a wink in Annabel's direction. "Great to finally meet you. I have heard so much about you. Annabel talks about you. A lot," she glanced at Annabel again, still wearing her roguish grin, and laughed.

David couldn't help but smile as his heart fluttered slightly. He already liked Julia. He looked nervously towards Annabel.

"I don't understand why you guys don't just spend more time together instead of just talking about each other to everyone..."

"How was the work in Wilmslow? Any interesting news?" Annabel interrupted her, changing the topic as swiftly and gracelessly as possible. Her face had gone slightly pinkish, and David felt his cheeks warming too.

Julia shook her head, "Nothing today. There were two girlfriends of City players discussing their holiday plans and their extravagant weddings. One of them was outraged that her fiancée asked for a prenup. Cried for almost the whole night. They're all the same, that lot – bag a rich ugly footballer, get married for a few years then bugger off and live off divorce payments and Instagram sponsorships for the rest of their lives."

Annabel laughed, rolling her eyes, "You're just jealous. Anyway, we have something a lot more exciting to talk about. Those guys on the train, the ones who wound up dead – they were after David," her tone was suddenly a lot more serious. Julia's eyebrows raised.

"What do you mean they were 'after' him?" she asked.

David began to fill Julia in on the events of the past twelve hours, before Annabel interrupted.

"It's clearly Anaia trying some of his dodgy tactics to throw David off of his game. You know about their dad, he was a seriously dodgy guy – I wouldn't put it past Ander and Marco to have some pretty serious contacts." Annabel's journalist nose twitched, it was clearly sensing a story. She and Julia had been working on a swamp-draining story about football corruption for years, and this sort of scandal would be a great link to tie everything together.

"Well, that's as may be, but then what bothers me is who the hell would kill those guys? Is it just a coincidence? Their pasts catching up with them, or is someone looking out for me?" said David.

"Maybe you've got someone on your side that we don't know about yet," she said reassuringly, "Whoever it was clearly knows what they're doing. I checked in with someone I know at the police station. These weren't gangland killings.

It was professional. A single bullet wound to the neck each. Fast, accurate. Deadly."

David still looked anxious, "You mean like a professional killer?" he stuttered, "I didn't see anyone following me other than the two Basque guys."

"If they're professional then that's probably why you didn't see them," Annabel said.

Julia interjected, "Well, I'd say it's fairly obvious that Anaia's involved, as you say. And didn't you tell me that someone called David earlier and told him to stay away? He wants to join the Table this summer, we know that. In my opinion he would do whatever it takes, he is capable of anything. And we certainly know what The Table is capable of…"

"The Table?" asked David, "Seriously? You're not telling me it's real?"

"You're better off not knowing," Annabel replied, shutting him down.

"Annabel," Julia looked at her from across the table, "If this really is Ander's doing, he's going to find out sooner or later. Better he hears it from us."

Annabel sighed and took a long sip from her glass. "Fine," she said, after another long pause, "but you can't say I didn't warn you."

24

As soon as she'd made it to the tree line, Joska had darted left and then right, and kept running until she thought her lungs would burst.

Over the uneven terrain, and having to dart in between trees, it was slow going and when she turned around, she could still vaguely see the outline of the hotel on the edge of the wood.

She sat down on a fallen trunk, panting, and tried to catch her breath. As she brought her breathing under control, she felt herself beginning to calm, felt her mind coming back to her. She was no longer a trapped animal in flight – if she was going to get out of this alive, she had to start to think.

She bent over and tightened the laces on the sneakers. They were too tight around the toes, but that was better than having a giant pair of clown shoes flapping about her feet. She took a closer look at them, at the red and green stripe cast diagonally across the stark white, the golden bee embroidered onto them, and longed for her running shoes.

Beggars can't be choosers, she told herself. Well, thieves, actually.

She heaved herself back up to standing and crept back the way she'd come. There was little point in keeping on running until she had her bearings, until she knew what she was running from, and that would be harder the further she got into the trees.

She thought back to what she'd seen in that room. It had been dark, gently lit by firelight, but that had been the only gentle thing about it. The majority of the people in the room had been women, but they were clearly in the service of the few men who were situated in the room on various furniture. Joska was no prude, but it was another thing entirely to be confronted by such a clear display of control and coercion. How many of the women in that room were there by choice?

And the worst thing was that she recognized some of the men. She had seen them at parties her dad had hosted. One man she remembered very clearly. He was tall, with a head like one of the statues on Easter Island and when she had met him, it felt like he'd gone out of his way to make her feel uncomfortable.

"My dear," he had said, as he picked up her outstretched hand and planted a kiss across her knuckles.

Joska shrank back and pulled her hand back, but he held on, subtly tightening his grip.

"You must get your looks from your mother, eh Ander?" he brought his hand up to the side of her face and traced a line from her temple down across her cheek, resting it on her shoulder. "Oh, to be young again."

Joska shuddered at the memory. She had felt his eyes on her the whole evening. Her dad had let her down that night. She knew he would never see her come to harm, but whatever that man had, her dad wanted so much that it had clouded all judgement. Was this what he was looking for?

Joska had reached the edge of the wood and looked back across to the hotel. There wasn't much sign of life. A valet sat playing on his phone, waiting for the next guests to arrive and a pair of bus boys busied themselves loading luggage into the rear of a limousine. Groundskeepers in green polo shirts and khaki shorts tended to the lawns and topiary.

As Joska began to relax, she noticed movement by the main entrance. Two men wearing dark suits emerged. One was a man-mountain. He was well over six and a half feet tall, and it felt to Joska like he was about the same widthways. Not fat, but pure muscle, he pushed against the seams of his clothing. He reminded her of one of the bulls she had seen at Las Ventas in Madrid. Her father was a proud Basque, but he had taken her to accompany him to the fight – if you could call it that – where he was trying to impress some work people. Come to think of it, she thought, had that man been there as well?

She had hated the event. Felt sorry for the bull, disgusted at the men who taunted it before killing, horrified at the crowds of her countrymen who had cheered as the poor animal bled out in front of them, calling out for its death. She had become a vegetarian that day, much to her father's disdain.

The man scanned the horizon and though Joska was well hidden, she instinctively flinched, pressing herself down into the ground. Her head lay on the floor, the smell of the earth, the mulch of leaves and fallen twigs filled her nostrils.

After a while, she twisted around and raised her head again. The second man she recognized immediately. It was the man who'd been keeping her down in the room in the basement. He had a cell phone to his ear and looked like he was giving orders.

He took the phone away and spoke to the first man, who nodded and turned his body away. Joska heard a sharp whistle and the man beckoned towards himself. Two men, dressed identically to the others, all in black, came trotting to the man-mountain and stood to attention. He spoke briefly, but Joska was too far away to make out anything anyone was saying. The two men nodded and stood up straight.

Her jailor, still on the phone, turned and made his way back inside the building as the other three spread a few metres apart and headed steadily for the trees.

They were coming for her.

Joska crawled backwards on her stomach, feeling the undergrowth smear against her legs and stomach, the damp of the rotting deadwood seeping through her thin cotton clothing. She shivered slightly, but kept low as she crawled back, turning and breaking into a crawl as she forced herself deeper into the woods. When she'd gone far enough, she stood up and ran.

This time she didn't stop when her lungs began to burn.

25

Ander had settled into his room on the tenth floor of his hotel and was sat comfortably in one of the grand lobby armchairs, enjoying a *kalimotxo.* The drink was reviving him. He had been working flat out all day to get this deal along the line, and now, with The Table using his daughter as leverage, he had to make sure he was firing on all cylinders.

He didn't think they would hurt her, but he knew the sort of games they liked to play. They operated outside of the normal rules of society.

He drained the last drops of his drink and stood up to leave, giving a nod of approval towards the bartenders.

When he had first visited the Radisson, the bartenders had never heard of the classic Basque cocktail. So, one night in the bar, after his brother had signed with Manchester United, he sat chatting with the staff, explaining the subtleties of the blend of red wine and Coke. It had to be Spanish wine, of course, and Original recipe Coca-Cola. Lots of ice, and a slice of lemon to serve, though Ander did sometimes opt for a slice of orange instead. He had visited the Radisson so many times that he no longer needed to order, as soon as he sat down, an ice cold *kalimotxo* was waiting at the table.

His phone rang.

"*Hola* Ander."

It was Markel.

Ander swallowed, the taste of *kalimotxo* still fresh on his tongue, "Hola Amigo. I have some very good news for you. I'm just waiting to hear the exact arrangements for your private jet. Get your stuff ready. The jet will fly you over within the next couple of hours," he paused, "if not, it will be no later than tomorrow morning."

"That's fantastic news, Ander," Markel sounded thrilled, "Dad had started to doubt you, but my trust never faltered."

"I told you I wouldn't disappoint you," Ander replied, puffing out his chest, inwardly maligning yet another parent meddling in the affairs of their talented offspring. "You know what? I'll make sure the plane is arranged for tonight. Then you can get some rest in Manchester tonight. You'll be in the same hotel as me."

"That would be amazing, thank you Ander. I'm very grateful."

"I'll call you back as soon as I've sorted it with the flight agency."

"Thanks Ander, thanks again."

Ander had been speaking with a concierge company in Monaco just in case Aitor had refused to organize the jet.

He called them again. Five minutes later, the jet was booked. Markel would arrive at the hotel just after 11pm in time for a proper night's sleep.

He arranged for a driver to pick Markel up from the airport and let the hotel staff know about the arrival of his special guest.

Ander felt good, things were coming together. Now he just needed to leak the information to his contact from MARCA. With the news out there, it would put even more pressure on the club, his brother and Aitor. Once the media had latched onto the story, it would be tougher to go back on it.

He walked back to his room and took a deep sigh of relief as he scanned his key card. The brief moment of relaxation was abruptly ended as his phone rang.

Typical, he thought. He rarely went more than half an hour without a phone call, especially on a day like today.

This time, surprisingly, it was Marco.

"Hi Ander," he sounded serious.

"Brother, is everything ok?"

"All good," he said, clearly hiding something, "Why don't you come for dinner at our place? I need to talk to you."

"Sounds good to me," he replied, hiding his anxiety. Why wouldn't Marco tell him over the phone? "I'll just have a quick shower, get dressed and then come over. Won't be any more than an hour. *Adios, hermanito*," said Ander and hung up.

It was odd that his brother would organise a sociable dinner on the penultimate night of the transfer window.

Everyone was even busier than usual, and the last time they spoke they'd hardly left on good terms.

He hoped that he wouldn't be forced to use the 'nuclear option' with Marco. He didn't want to destroy his brother's family, but there was a lot more riding on this deal now than just a hefty chunk of commission.

He slumped onto his hotel bed, checking the latest football news. The headline that he'd fed out to the press had made the front page.

Ander smirked. It was time to call upon another friend.

"Mr. Anaia, how are you? I assume you need something from me?"

"I'm good, my friend. There's no getting past you, is there?" Ander laughed, "I need to see you tonight please. Its urgent. Come to my hotel at about 10pm. Come straight to the club lounge on the tenth floor but be careful not to be seen."

The other man hesitated. "Alright," he said, "See you later."

As soon as the call disconnected, Ander was dialling another number. His plan was picking up momentum.

"Ander, good to hear your voice, it's been a while. Are you in town again? The last time I saw you was at that party you organised. What a night! When's the next one?"

Ander knew the way to John's heart. He had organized a party the previous year, to which he had invited a few select journalists. Ones he knew would hold their tongues in exchange for extravagances they couldn't imagine in their wildest dreams. The drinks had flowed freely, and the women that Ander had paid to attend had made pains to ensure everyone he had invited was made very comfortable.

The selection committee of The Table had also been there. There had always been rumours about The Table – an elite set of football folk who ruled the game from the shadows with extreme prejudice, whilst pushing the limits of excess and personal gratification – but no one had any idea if they were true, let alone who was a member. When Ander had been approached, he hadn't been particularly surprised. He had a track record of hosting lavish parties, and his record of deal-breaking was spoken about throughout the industry. He wasn't afraid to use dirty tactics to get what he wanted, and this is what had attracted the attention of The Table.

He was able to manipulate people seemingly to his will. He seemed to understand the basest desires of anyone he spoke to and was able to use this to his advantage to get exactly what he wanted. Whether that was through complicity or blackmail depended on the reaction of the other person. Ander's black book was extensive, which was why he also liked to keep a posse of journalists on hand to do his bidding when required.

"I'm planning a big one after the transfer window. On a yacht off the coast of Ibiza. A week full of nice wine, sunshine and whatever else you might like. How does that sound?"

"It sounds like I need to pack my stuff," said John, chuckling. Ander knew he would be unable to resist.

"Well, I need to see you tonight first. First, though, I need you to drop a bit of news for me please."

"Anything you need." Ander was a little repulsed by John's eagerness to please but grunted his approval.

"It's about the player from Germany; the one coming in for the medical at United tomorrow. I noticed he had an injury almost a year ago which ruled him out for about six months. I need you to create a problem out of it."

"Got you," John replied, "Will take me about 15 minutes to get the story out."

"Great. One more detail, though. I need you to add that Aitor is trying to push this deal over the line, despite the medical issues. Make it clear that the owners in the US wouldn't be happy at all," Ander paused, he wanted to make sure this article served its purpose, "Oh," he remembered, "And also highlight the fact that Aitor is the brother-in-law of Andoni and that everyone close to Manchester and their board disapprove of the situation. It doesn't look good for the club."

"Don't worry, Ander. Just leave it with me. See it as done. I'll sink Aitor so deep they'll need a submarine to find him again."

They laughed together.

"Great John. That man was a waiter in Bilbao before Andoni knocked up his sister. Now he directs the biggest club in England and one of the biggest in the world. Not many fans would be happy with that if they knew."

"Noted, I will send you the link asap. I'll see you at the hotel later."

Ander needed to get ready for Marco's but made one final call. Miller clearly hadn't taken the hint from his interaction on the train. He needed to send a clearer message.

He pulled out his burner line. He had sourced a case of old Nokia handsets and pay-as-you-go SIM cards from a contact who had helped him supply "entertainment" at one of his parties a few years ago.

He selected the only number in the contacts list. After a few rings, the line connected.

"Do we have further business?" In truth, Ander hated talking to these people. They were rough, primed for violence at all times. They always seemed so happy to take on more opportunity to intimidate people, to hurt them. It disgusted Ander, but they had their uses.

"We need to take it up a notch. The message hasn't quite hit home." Ander was careful not to be explicit on the phone. You could never be too careful.

"Understood. Who?"

"Let's keep this away from family for now," A pang of despair hit him as he tried to imagine where Joska was, how she was feeling. He had no doubt that they would have mentioned him, how her capture was his fault. It would take a big person to forgive him. He hoped that he could do something to convince Joska that she could. She was a good person. Not like him.

"His offices are in Mayfair," Ander snapped back to the matter at hand, packing his emotions away to be confronted at a more appropriate time. This was business. "Perhaps take a visit."

Ander gave the address of Miller's offices and hung up the phone. If this didn't work, he didn't know where he could go next with him. It would mean that he'd have to lean on his brother harder than he had to get this deal across the line. To get to The Table. To get Joska home.

26

Annabel had finished her drink and called someone over to order another round.

As they waited for the drinks to arrive, she posed a question.

"What would spring to mind if I mentioned The Table, David?"

"Oh, that old chestnut? Some tin-foil hat conspiracy about a secret cabal who rule the world of football?" David had inherited his German mother's pragmatism and rationality. "It's a load of nonsense, isn't it? Invented by boring people trying to inject a little spice into their mundane lives? In fact, wasn't David Icke a goalkeeper – it was probably him who started it. Are you going to tell me that Alex Ferguson is a lizard?" David's grin was fading as he noticed Annabel and Julia's serious faces.

"At the risk of sounding melodramatic," Annabel's voice was quiet but forceful, "Keep your voice down. You never know who's listening." She nodded over to the bar area and David noticed a group of middle-aged men dressed in United training kit. Coaching staff, David concluded.

Julia shifted uncomfortably in her seat. She wasn't used to being so exposed. There were people around who she recognized, having tracked them, dived into their histories, their personal lives. She knew their truths, and their secrets.

Annabel continued as Julia buried her head into a drinks menu.

"The Table is very real, and it's what I… what we have been tracking over these past few years. Initially, I was planning to write an expose of nepotism in the industry. I'd seen the power the Anaia brothers wielded, how it was negatively affecting the game, but it wasn't the first case. There's still a story to be had there. But this is bigger. Much bigger."

Annabel had leaned in as she was talking, keeping her voice low and David had unwittingly mimicked her. Their heads were almost touching, their eyes locked.

Before she could continue, a waiter arrived with a tray of drinks and placed them down on the table. David passed Annabel and Julia theirs and took a sip from his soda water. He fished into his wallet and handed the waiter a tip; the boy looked as though all his Christmases had come at once.

"But Anaia is the link. That's why I've been following your deal so closely. That's why this thing on the train is such a big deal. I think this deal is his ticket to The Table." David couldn't believe what Annabel was saying. He glanced over to Julia, but she just gave him a slight nod, confirming everything Annabel was saying.

"But his luck's run out at United – the head honchos have decreed from on high that they don't want Ander's player. He's made promises that he can't keep, but he's going to try every dirty trick in the book to ensure he wins."

"Like threatening me on the train," David final managed to get a word in.

"Exactly," the men at the bar had moved off and Julia had re-joined the conversation, "I've been following Ander for a year or two now. The guy's a bully. I bet he's got more dirt on people that I have. Loves to throw a lavish party – drink, drugs, women. All it would take would be a secret camera somewhere and you'd have the keys to the city. If he wants to join The Table, that information is his ticket – he can control the Premiership. Place players where he wants. Once you can do that, you can start playing the bookies. Power, money – that's all he wants and that's exactly what they can give him."

This was the most David had heard Julia speak. She was less excitable than Annabel. Her tone was calm, measured. Authoritative. The mixture of Annabel's enthusiasm and Julia's down-the-line attitude meant he was rapidly coming around to their way of thinking.

"But where's the danger of The Table? Sure, there are some dodgy blokes who like to host hedonistic parties – but that comes with the territory. Money and power beget money and power."

"We have a good sense now of a few people who might sit at The Table. Julia spotted them at one of Anaia's parties," Annabel had picked up the conversation again, "There are several incidents we think we can link to their meddling. Sex scandals, failed drugs tests, and more worryingly there have been some instances where players have picked up injuries off the field or the training ground. The Table manipulates the whole game – it's not just agents playing hardball to get their commissions, we're talking big league gambling. Millions resting on whether a player signs for this team or that team..." As if on cue, David's phone rang. He raised a finger apologetically to Annabel and Julia and got up out of his seat.

"Patrick!" he put on his warmest voice, "Have you landed? How was the flight?"

"Hi David, yes we're here. I'm just getting into the car and then I think we're going to go into town to get some food before making our way to the hotel. I've not eaten since breakfast."

"Great! Well, I'm already at the hotel waiting for you. Take as long as you like. Enjoy the city. Listen, Patrick, I'm just in the middle of looking through a final contract thing, I'll see you when you get here?" David hated lying to his client, but he wanted to hear more from Annabel and Julia about The Table. He'd thought it was all a big joke at first, but the more they explained, the more plausible it seemed. They were serious women, they weren't going to hinge their careers on some conspiracy. If they managed to break this story, it would make them.

"Does Patrick know about anything that's been going on?" asked Julia when he returned to the table.

"No, he doesn't," replied David, "But I that's for the best. He just needs to focus on his football."

"Definitely wise," said Annabel.

"So…" David continued, "The Table really exists?"

"Yes, and it goes a lot deeper, a lot darker than a few scandalous photos and a push down the stairs. They're not just involved in manipulating the game, there's a considerably darker side to things."

"I don't think I want to know," David said.

"You don't," Annabel had lost her prior enthusiasm and was solemn now. "You really don't."

27

"We'll keep looking, boss, but she's got the jump on us. She could have gone in any direction," the man explained, "We're miles away from anything remotely like civilization here and there's only one road down the mountain. I've posted a couple of boys halfway down. They'll pick her up, but I say we just leave it. She's half-naked. When the temperature drops, she'll be forced to make a move. We'll pick her up then."

The older man stared at him from behind a monolithic mahogany desk. The curtains in the vast room had been partially drawn, sapping the midday sun of its power and casting everything in the room in chiaroscuro.

He raised his eyebrows, "Thank you so much for your expert opinion, Micha" he didn't try to hide the sarcasm in his voice, "But I would prefer you to do what I've fucking told you to do. Get back out there and find the little troublemaker. She has seen our faces. She cannot be allowed to leave."

Micha knew better than to argue. He'd seen what happened to those who did. Had been the one to make it happen in some cases.

"Yes, sir, I've still got people out there looking. What do you want us to do when we find her?" he asked.

The other man was silent for a moment, his gaze fixed on something far away. A malicious smile passed across his face.

"Bring her back here. I'm sure we can think of something – her father has yet to make good on his promises to us." He opened a drawer in the desk, finding nothing but dust and some complementary stationery. He took out the paper and began sketching idly. "Of course, now she's seen who we are, what we can do, she can't ever be allowed to leave, even if he does tie up his deal."

Micah almost felt sorry for the girl. None of this was her doing but look where she'd ended up. If she'd have just stuck where she was, she'd almost be on her way home. Now she was out in the wilderness with just the clothes on her back.

Anaia knew the people he was dealing with. Your place at the table was bought with more than just cash. If this was anyone's fault, it was his.

"Do you need anything else?" the man sat at the desk spoke sharply to Micah, breaking him out of his thoughts.

"Nothing, boss. I'll check back in with you in the next hour or s—"

"Don't bother," the man interrupted. Micah looked down at the desk to where the man was still doodling. Thick, black, jagged marks were scored hard around the edge of the paper, breaking off over the page into hypnotic spirals which layered over each other. "I don't need updates, I need you to find her. Don't waste any more time than has already been lost."

Without another word, Micah turned and left the room, glad to emerge from the gloom into the hallway outside.

"So?" asked a giant of a man who'd been waiting for him outside.

"Call everyone in. Get back into the woods. Three man teams, a full sweep. Make sure they overlap. We find her before sunset."

28

Ander sniffed his shirt as he walked towards his brother's door. He smelt fresh, he'd showered and sprayed himself with his new cologne before leaving the hotel. He felt tense, anticipating the argument he was going to have to have with his brother. He enjoyed using strongarm tactics with others, but Marco was still his brother. He didn't want to have to use malicious means to get his way, but he would. He reminded himself that there was more than just the glory of the deal and the fulfilment of his desire to join The Table.

He thought of Joska. Did he want to be part of a group who would do this to his own blood? He understood that it was a test of his commitment, but it hurt that he'd unwittingly put his daughter in this position. He thought of the other women who he'd seen at the parties. He'd always told himself they were just willing participants; hangers on willing to do anything for a taste of the high life. Had ignored the reality he knew was lurking underneath.

Ander shook himself back to the present. He had to focus completely on the conversation he was anticipating with Marco. He had to be careful to let his brother know he was serious about letting the information leak, but he didn't want to let the cat out of the bag too early to Maria. It was his trump card and he needed to keep it hidden for as long as he could. Perhaps he would never need to use it.

He rang the doorbell, heard a frantic scuffle, and muffled shouting from inside. The door sprung open as his nephews threw themselves at him. He pulled them into a bear hug.

He had a very strong bond with his nephews. He always looked forward to the special moment they shared when he saw them for the first time after being in Spain for a while.

He was their only uncle; Maria didn't have any siblings. This had given Ander a great feeling of responsibility. He and Joska had become close in the last few years, but his work had taken him away from the family home a lot when she was young. He hadn't been around a lot when she was younger – his work, and the extracurricular activities that surrounded it had enticed him away. In some way, the attention he paid to his nephews was his attempt to rebalance the universe.

"Bienvenido, Ander," said Maria, her unwelcoming frown seemed far out of place from the big grins on her sons' faces.

"Hola Maria," replied Ander, the warmth he'd contrived on their earlier meeting was completely gone now. He walked past Maria to look for his brother, handing her his coat.

He made his way into the kitchen and poured himself a glass of wine from the carafe that was sitting on the counter. Maria followed him into the kitchen, giving him an ice cold stare. She went to say something, but clearly thought better of it and started making the final preparations for dinner.

"Smells amazing, Maria," Ander reassumed his fake sincerity, "So, boys, where's your dad?"

As he asked the question, he heard Marco coming down the stairs.

"Brother, welcome," the tension in the room was palpable. Clearly Maria had told Marco about their earlier interaction, and Ander was certain that Marco would have discussed their dealings earlier that day. Part of it, at least, he thought, letting a smile snake across his face.

Marco turned to his sons, who were roughhousing in the hallway.

"Boys, enough! Bed," he commanded, with a knowing smile, "Remember to brush your teeth."

Marco approached his brother, and there was a brief, hostile embrace between them, before the Anaia brothers and Maria moved into the dining room and sat down at the table. Maria removed the lids from the dishes in front of them.

Ander was shocked. Each dish was piled high with traditional Basque food; he had never seen anything near 'home food' in this house before. The dishes included all of his all-time favourites and they looked cooked to perfection.

He was gobsmacked that Maria had managed to cook all of this. The most he'd ever seen her prepare in the kitchen was toast. He was impressed.

"Maria, you dark horse! When did you learn to cook all of this?" As he began to speak, he heard footsteps approaching from the kitchen. He turned to look, and he had to double take. He couldn't believe it; this was even more of a surprise than the food.

"Come, sit here Ama," said Marco, pulling out the chair next to him.

"Ama?" Ander gasped, "But how? When? Why?"

"Hola, my son. It's so good to see you," she said, embracing him in his chair before walking around to sit next to Marco, "I arrived a few hours ago. Just in time to cook my boys their favourite food. Did Marco not tell you I was coming?"

Her warm, ear-to-ear smile filled Ander with a strange, childish happiness. Just seeing her gave him a brief feeling that everything was going to be okay.

"I had no idea!" he said through his unerasable grin, "Why did you come over so suddenly? I only left this morning; you should have come with me!"

She paused, glancing to Marco on the seat beside her. Ander raised an eyebrow, waiting for her to continue, "Your brother needed to speak to me about something important and wanted me to come over today."

Ander suddenly didn't feel so comfortable. Something strange was going on here. Why would his mother come over with less than a day's notice? She barely ever left their small town.

Ander couldn't believe Marco would do this. Use their own mother in this way. He knew that Ander was a 'mummy's boy'; he had never been able to cope when their mother was sad or ill. Ander would never do something to make her unhappy and do almost anything to keep her happy. He was planning on manipulating Ander through his mother.

He glared at Marco, "So then brother, what is so important that you had to bring our poor mother all this way away from home in a private jet? Today of all days as well!" he exclaimed "This really must be important."

Marco wasn't amused. He glanced gravely at his mother and Ander before seeming to look to his wife for reassurance.

"I should have told you this a while ago and I owe you all an explanation," started Marco, his intense gaze never shifted from his wife as he spoke. "It's something that I want you to hear from me. All together. My family."

Marco took another deep breath as his wife nodded slowly. Ander's heart raced. Perhaps he had misunderstood Marco's intent. His mother sat silently, preparing herself for a hammer blow.

"I have cancer," said Marco bluntly as he looked solemnly down at his plate.

There was an excruciating silence around the table, broken only by the muffled snivelling of his wife and mother. Both were trying to mask their crying but to no avail.

Ander felt a lump in his throat but forced his tears back. Everything fell into perspective. For once, Ander was lost for words as his mind plunged into a whirlwind of thoughts.

I was going to expose him to the family for his affair. I was threatening him. What was I doing? My brother is dying, and I was about to use his affair for my gain. He must have been desperate. Ander silently admonished himself. His greed had forced him to lose perspective completely.

The deathly silence still lay over the table.

Marco glanced up nervously, the whole room waited for him to speak. He took a deep breath, gently cleared his throat and began to speak with a grave softness, "I know you must all have a lot of questions. I'm sorry I haven't told you before, but I never wanted you guys to be affected by it and brought down into my world of sadness. I only found out a year ago, I have fought against it, and I am still fighting. It's prostate cancer."

A small gasp came from Maria's chair. Marco looked towards her; their eyes locked in a tearful gaze. He had to look away before he could carry on. Ander couldn't believe he hadn't even told his wife.

"The times that I've been staying late at the training ground were for my treatment. Sometimes I couldn't muster the strength to come home because I was overwhelmed with guilt. My excuse was always working hard. Which was true, I always worked hard, and it has never affected my job. I just wanted to keep it away from you."

Ander placed his arm around their mother as she choked into a sob she failed to hide.

"Only two people from the management know about my condition. I realised I had to tell you all last week after a couple of other people questioned my health. I know the rumours will come out soon and it might hit the news. I wanted you guys to hear it from me rather than anywhere else. All along I planned to tell you when I was cancer free. I wanted to beat it myself but unfortunately there is still a long way to go."

His mother did her best to compose herself. She had no time to gather her thoughts. "My little son. I love you so much," she mustered, the first thing that came to her mind.

"I love you too, mum," Marco whispered painfully as his mum leaned over to comfort his wife.

"I can't believe you didn't tell me..."

Tears rolled down Maria's cheeks. Her words caught in her throat.

Ander broke the echoes of sobs, "You should have told us, brother. We are your family. We would have been there for you from the start. You didn't have to go through this all by yourself."

Marco nodded slowly, "I know, I know. But I was thinking about you, not myself. Seeing you guys unhappy would have been more devastating for me than fighting cancer alone."

Marco's selflessness hit Ander hard. He was ashamed for what he had tried to do. He couldn't stay there any longer. He needed to leave.

While his little brother was fighting cancer alone, he was threatening him with his affair for his own success.

Ander rose silently from the table and left the house, staring at the floor as his family watched him leave. His mind was flooded with guilt. He had been prepared to destroy the family he cherished so much by exposing the affair. This was not who he was. He had to leave.

Outside, gasping lungfuls of air, Ander scanned the street desperately searching for a cab. Out of luck, he pulled out his phone. Before he could open up an app to order a cab, his phone lit up with a call. He didn't need this now, but he needed to answer.

The line connected, the voice on the other end didn't bother with pleasantries.

"I sent you two guys to help deal with your stupid football business and now they're dead. Two of my best people."

Ander was completely confused.

"What's going on?" The last he'd heard, the plan to scare Miller off had worked.

"Do you not read the fucking news? They're dead. Murdered on the same train that your man was on. I don't know whether he's involved or not, but he's a dead man walking." The man's voice was completely calm, measured. It terrified Ander.

"I'm going to find out who's done this. I've sent over two more people. My best. They just arrived in Manchester. They'll head directly to the hotel and finish what we started. There's nothing worse than unfinished business."

"Just hold on a minute, I need your help. There's something more important now. They have my daughter. I need you to help me find h—"

"The time for helping you is through, Ander, my boy. We're done. The debt to your father was paid a long time ago." The man cut him off. He was in no mood for negotiation. "I think you are staying in the same hotel, yes? Remember to say hello." He let out a laugh that sounded like crunching gravel. "No, no! what are you doing? I wasn't told about this. Send them back," Ander was flustered and panicking, "People will find out. Two Basque people died this afternoon and now you've sent two more! Are you crazy? No one else needs to get hurt. This was just to scare them off the deal. That's it, it's gone too far!"

"I lost two men," the voice replied stubbornly, "I have unfinished business. I will fix this."

The phone line went dead.

29

"Are you coming, mate?" William was pulling on his Burberry trench coat, slapping his pockets and crossing off his mental checklist: keys, wallet, phone.

"*Si, si* – just give me thirty seconds to finish this," Jose's eyes were squinting at the screen. It had been a long day, they'd both barely moved from their laptops all day as they double and triple-checked everything David had sent through.

William slumped down into the sofa. It seemed ridiculous, to fit the battered old oxblood Chesterfield into such a small office – it had seemed especially so as they had tried to navigate it up the narrow staircase when they'd moved in – but it had been the sofa they'd had in their first student house and had followed them ever since.

As he sank down into the worn leather cushions, William pulled out his phone and started idly browsing the internet as he waited for Jose to finish.

"Shit, Jose – have you seen this thing about the ETA guys? Two men found dead on a train going to Manchester. Executed gangland style, it looks like. Professional job."

"Hm..." Jose wasn't paying attention as he scrolled his mouse, the pages on pages of text moving in front of his eyes, blurring into one.

"Didn't you say something about David being threatened by two blokes, all tatted up, shaved heads and that?"

Jose's curiosity was piqued now. He saved what he was doing and turned to William, pinching the bridge of his nose, his eyes screwed shut.

"It does seem like quite the coincidence. There can't be many Basque separatists floating around Stockport." Jose was smiling. He kept his eyes closed, grateful for the break from the glare of the screen.

"But really, if it was those men who threatened David then... not to seem too blunt about it, but they won't be doing much more of that, will they?"

William took a moment to register Jose's blunt reaction. He had to admit, Jose had a point.

"You don't think it was Davey, do you?" he was only half joking. He'd never known someone quite so determined to get what they want. But David was too much of a good guy, he wouldn't hurt a fly.

Jose burst into laughter.

"My friend, that is the laugh I needed after this long day. Come, let us away, as they say. Your round."

He closed the lid of his laptop and grabbed his things and the two left the office, punching in the alarm code and deadlocking the door behind them.

It was still warm outside, the late August sun still warming their corner of Mayfair. They had missed rush hour, and the crowds on the street were strictly there to party. Groups of men and women made their way through Mayfair in their finery, heading for the latest hotspots to be seen in.

"Where to then?" William asked Jose, hoping that his friend would forget his upmarket proclivities and opt for somewhere simple and unassuming where they could sink a few pints, talk about football, not talk about football contracts, and get some chips on the way home.

"Soho? What about French House?" So much for unassuming, but William did quite like the Breton cider and perhaps they could tuck themselves away in a corner somewhere for a bit.

They crossed Regents Street, not bothering to wait for the lights to change as they weaved their way between the traffic. They walked past Liberty, William willing Jose past the window displays, distracting his friend from his shopping habit.

Heading down Great Marlborough Street, the friends assumed the sort of companionable silence that only occurred between two people completely comfortable with one another. They cut down Berwick Street, William now having to be dragged away from the front of the record stores. It was his Achilles heel, and after the basics were paid for, most of his money went on music. He eschewed fancy clothes and lavish restaurants for hi-fi equipment and vinyl.

As they reached the French House, William's plans for a quiet night were blown out of the water completely. They were hit by a wall of sound, hundreds of people blowing off steam after a long week. He looked across to Jose, who wore a cheeky grin. Jose raised his eyebrows, a challenge to William, as though he knew what was going through his friend's head.

"Fine," William said, resigned, a smile spreading across his lips.

Jose clapped him on the back and pushed him forward into the throng of revellers, becoming one with the crowd.

They had left the French House after Jose had gotten into an argument with the landlord about using his phone – there was a strict 'no tech' policy in the bar – and had rolled deeper into Soho. A few quiet pints had rapidly descended into many loud ones, until the two friends found themselves three sheets to the wind, queuing for chips outside a kebab shop on Oxford Street.

"I'm telling you, Celtic could easily compete with the top four in the EPL!" Jose was shaking his head at his friend, his body shaking softly as he laughed.

"William, seriously? Next you'll be trying to convince me that Robertson and Tierney are the best full backs in the world."

"Who says they're not? Did you see them completely shut down England at the Euros? And, much as it pains me, that's an England side that went on to the finals!" William's determination was growing with each of his friend's comebacks.

They moved forwards to the counter and placed their orders. Minutes later, they were back outside working their way towards the tube. As they reached the top of the steps, Jose patted at his pockets.

"What's up?" William asked.

"I don't have my keys." As he said it, he could picture exactly where they were on his desk. "I'm going to have to go back and get them – I gave the spare to the cleaner and I've not got another one cut yet." He bunched up the rest of his chip packet and sent it in an arc towards a nearby bin.

"Want me to come with you?" William noticed the chip wrapper completely miss the bin, landing several feet wide.

"No, no, it's fine – you get home. It's another long day tomorrow. I'll get a cab back."

"Here, take my office key," said William, unwinding the key from its chain.

"Thank you. Get home safe," Jose said, wrapping his friend in a brief, strong embrace.

"See you on the morrow – bright and early!" cried William as he made his way down the steps into the station.

Jose pulled up his collar and plugged his earbuds in, cranking up the music on his phone. The clear night had invited a chill to the air, and the warm jacket of alcohol had started to wane as he faced the sobering reality of having to go back to the office. Maybe he'd just sleep there, he thought, as he pounded the pavement back past the swathes of partygoers falling out of nightclubs into waiting cabs.

The square was closed at this time of night, so he skirted the edge, fishing for the key to the front door in his pocket. He bobbed his head rhythmically to the music that filled his head. As he pushed the key into the lock, he noticed a shadow cast over the door. Something was blocking out the street light behind him. As he turned his head, he felt cold metal press against his cheek. He froze, his hand resting on the key in the door.

"*Barruan*," a voice like a low rumble of thunder demanded. Inside. "Now."

30

David, Annabel, and Julia had carried on drinking in the bar. David had switched to drinking beer a while ago, and the three were talking animatedly about Annabel and Julia's investigations into nepotism in football.

"The Catholic Church?" David was looking at Annabel, confused.

Annabel nodded, and continued "Well, the word Nepotism originally referred to the assignment of nephews to important positions by Catholic Popes and bishops. Historically, nepotism plagued the Catholic Church for centuries," she explained.

"So, the Popes would put their nephews into a position that helped him become the next Pope?" asked David.

"Meaning power was based on bloodlines and relationships, rather than merit," added Julia, "One of the biggest examples was Callixtus III, head of the Borgia family. He made two of his nephews cardinals. One of them, Rodrigo, used the position as a steppingstone to the papacy, becoming Pope Alexander VI. Alexander then elevated

Alessandro Farnese, his mistress's brother, to cardinal. He would later become Pope Paul III."

"But the Popes were a little too high up to get away with it regularly. It was mainly the bishops. It was one of the factors that led to legislation around celibacy in the Catholic Church and the Protestant Reformation."

David nodded, slightly lost as to how they had gone from discussing murder on a train to Catholicism. He wasn't going to interrupt; clearly, Annabel and Julia were enjoying getting into their subject.

"That's unbelievable, why didn't I ever hear about that," said David, shaking his head in disbelief.

"So, how does this all link back to football then?" he eventually filled the silence.

"Well, it really all started at the end of the eighties at United. The new manager granted favours to family members and friends by using his position and power to benefit them."

"Wait," said David, "Alex Ferguson?"

"Sir Alex Ferguson, David," Annabel smiled.

"So, the Basque brothers aren't the first in the premiership to be doing this?"

"David," Annabel smirked at his naivety, "They're not even the first at United! So, Sir Alex got his brother Martin the job as chief European Scout. He was in the job until his brother retired. For sixteen years he was on the payroll, monitoring players in mainland Europe," explained Annabel.

"But what exactly is the problem with that?" asked David, "He was a player and coach, wasn't he? It's hardly an unusual career path. And he had some big hits in his time? Forlan,

Anderson, van Nistelrooy — looks like he did a decent enough job to me."

It felt like Annabel had a prepared answer for anything David threw at her. She'd been working on this story, alongside the one about The Table for over a year. She had all her bases covered. "But it's unusual to become a chief scout without any experience. It's even more unusual to become a chief scout for the biggest club in England. Unless your brother is Sir Alex. The question is not whether he was a good scout or not. It's a question of ethics and fairness. The issue is that he was promoted into such a big role only because of his brother. He was an average lower league player and an unsuccessful coach. He would never have got the role normally, and that is fact. In fact, before 1997, there was no such thing as the 'Chief European scout' for United — it's almost as if they created the role just for him. Then there's Alex's son, Darren..."

"He played for United, didn't he?" asked David, taking the words from Annabel's mouth.

"He was picked for the first team in place of Bryan Robson." Julia had taken up the mantle now. "Guess who picked him?" she asked rhetorically.

"Everyone must have known he wasn't good enough but who could argue with the boss?" David added in disbelief.

More drinks arrived. The bar was fairly empty now. David checked his watch. It wouldn't be too long now until Patrick arrived. David hoped that Patrick wouldn't notice he'd been drinking too much.

"Everyone would give their own son the same opportunity. Wouldn't you guys do the same? I don't think that is illegal."

"None of this is illegal," continued Julia, "But it's unethical, especially when other players didn't get the same opportunity." It was hard to disagree with that.

"Manchester United was not a family business owned by the Fergusons," Annabel said, "It's a public company. The bottom line is that Ferguson was just an employee. He shouldn't have been able to abuse his power and position to gift opportunities to his family members and friends," she said. She was angry, barely holding back her rage at the injustice. Annabel had not been born with a silver spoon in her mouth. She had grown up on one of the worst estates in Manchester, raised by her grandparents. She had worked incredibly hard to get to where she was. David could understand her annoyance where others were gifted their status and privilege.

"But surely it depends on each case?" As much as he understood her, he wasn't sure it was quite as clear cut as she saw it. "If the son of a coach is, on merit, good enough to play for the club then he should be able to. In fact, it might even be more difficult for them because expectations would be higher than usual," David said, "There would be added pressure from all camps. Everyone would be watching."

"Perfectly valid point," Annabel admitted, "But that's not what's happening. Nepotism has a firm grip throughout the industry and it's risking ruining the game. Mancini signed his two sons at Man City. Anthony Pulis—"

"You mean Tony Pulis, the coach?" asked David.

Annabel caught her breath. "I thought you might say that" she said, clapping her hands and rubbing them together, "The Tony we all know and love signed one player three times. Anthony. His son. There's more. Johan and Jordi Cruyff; Garry and Lee Johnson; Ronnie and Ian Thomas-Moore; Paul and Blair Sturrock. It's all over the place, and that's just English clubs. There are cases all of Europe where the same thing's happening."

Annabel's voice had risen a few decibels and the few people left nursing their drinks were glancing in their direction."

"Look at Bayern!" continued Annabel, "Rummenige's family has all sorts of ties to the club. His son's an agent. His brother is a partner at Schwarzer and Rummenigge."

"It must be so difficult for an agent to be involved with the club's deals if your brother is the President," David joked.

"It's not just the Rummenigge family either, there's the Hoeneß family as well. They run under the radar by partnering with other agencies. Sebastian was a coach at the academy for years and now runs the first team. It's not just restricted to football either. One of the sons runs a sausage business in Nurnberg. Guess where the Allianz Arena gets their sausages from?"

The three of them chuckled in disbelief at the ridiculousness of it all.

"So, if nepotism is so rife, and it seems like it started at United, surely the Anaia brothers are as thick as thieves?"

David brought the conversation back to the matter at hand. "It doesn't make sense, then, that Ander would be putting pressure on me to get his deal across the line. Surely it's in the bag if Marco's on his side?"

"Ah," said Annabel, "Therein lies the rub. Rumour has it that the owners in the US have had enough of Ander. For too long, he's been placing bad players at the club – which Marco has facilitated – and it's started to affect the fans view of United. Bad vibes from the supporters mean fewer ticket and merch sales. To them it's nothing more than a business, and Ander's costing them money. The buck stops with Marco, and I heard that they've relegated his player way down the list. Patrick's at the top, of course."

David felt a swell of pride, though he knew there was a lot of luck involved in his finding Patrick, and for Patrick signing and staying with him. Soon it would all pay off, he told himself.

"And then this links to The Table because you think Ander's promised them results?" David felt naïve sat between these two women who'd devoted their lives to this story over the past few years.

Annabel scoffed, "He will try to use his brother to push his own deal. He will do anything to succeed. He wants to join the Table at all costs. I do wonder, though, if he knows what he's signing up for. The Table is involved in more than just football."

"With this much money at play, there's a long list of horrible things they're involved with. I don't even really want to talk about it," Julia said.

"I'm sure you can imagine, David. Wealthy men who are used to getting everything they want, with the power and influence to keep it all hidden," added Annabel.

David looked horrified.

"So, it really exists..." Like everyone he'd ever met, he had always assumed it was some kind of mythical organization.

"It was founded nearly twenty-five years ago. It was a response to the Bosman ruling. Clubs could no longer block a move or demand a fee if a player left after their contract had expired."

"Free agents," David was well aware of the significance of the Bosman ruling.

"Exactly," continued Annabel, "But it also created a big opportunity for agents. They started demanding signing-on fees and commission because clubs didn't need to pay a transfer fee for a free agent anymore, they had more money to give to the players and the agents instead of the releasing club. The power in negotiations shifted from the clubs to the players and their agents. A group of powerful agents came together and created The Table.

At first it was a platform from which they could collaborate to be a stronger and more successful force in the transfer market. It was a way of controlling and influencing players and clubs to allow the agents to do as they pleased.

They drummed up a world of superyacht parties filled with supermodels to invite club officials to and gave out lavish gifts and cash payments to ensure they got what they wanted.

But of course, what they then started to do was collect information on people. They set themselves up as facilitators of desire. We all know how quickly that sort of thing can turn dark, and it did. And they made sure they had a paper trail – they could change overnight from the people who could get you laid, to those who could destroy your family overnight. They essentially blackmail their way to the top, and no one has the balls to do anything about it because of their own self-interest.

"Well, that's what me and Julia are setting out to change. It's gone on too long, too many people have been hurt." Annabel was squeezing the arms of her chair so hard her knuckles had turned white.

"The Table is ruled by Jack Farmington," Julia let the name hang in the air.

"Farmington?" Jack Farmington was known by everybody in football. A former criminal, he had spent time in prison before becoming an agent.

"The very same," said Annabel, "And now the sole Spanish member has retired, the door has opened for another Spanish agent to fill the gap."

"That's where Ander comes in," it was all clicking into place for David now.

"It's between him and one more person. Ander must need the deal tomorrow or he'll be out the race.

"It sounds more like a cartel than an agency," said David, only half joking.

"Yep, it does and a very powerful cartel at that," nodded Annabel.

"So, Ander is against the ropes – Marco's looking like he's not going to be swayed by Ander this time, which means Ander's not going to get his place at the table. It makes sense, then, that he'd be the one who tried to scare me off," said David.

"But then how did those guys end up dead? If they're working for Ander, who's trying to stop him? The other agent?"

"Could be," conceded Annabel, "But I don't actually think that's the most important thing at the moment. I think what we need to keep in mind is that Ander's not going to stop. If those guys were working for him, there'll be more. You have to be careful, David – promise me." She reached out and touched his hand, her eyes meeting his. She seemed genuinely concerned for him.

"I will, but there's no way I'm not going to go through with my deal. Ander's a bully, and sometimes the only way to get a bully to stop is to punch back." He surprised himself with how strongly he felt. He saw Annabel sink slightly and cast her eyes towards Julia.

"Men..." Julia sank the rest of her drink, "I need to go – Annabel, can I get a ride?"

"Of course," Annabel took her hand off of David's and packed her things into her bag. She fished some notes out of her purse.

"No, don't worry, I've got this," It was the least David could do after the thorough education he'd received from them both.

"Thanks," Annabel said, Julia was already heading for the lobby. David leaned forwards and put his arm around her in a friendly embrace, planting a small kiss on her cheek.

"It was great seeing you," he said, "Let me know if you're free at the end of the week. It would be great to catch up properly, once all this is over."

"Sure, David," Annabel said, "That would be nice." She gave him a small, sad smile. "I mean it, David. Be careful with this. I want you to get this deal as much as anyone else, but I don't want to see you get hurt. It's not worth it."

David took her hand now, "I promise."

"Goodbye David," Annabel said, "Say hello to Patrick for me. I'll see you first thing in the morning. I'll make some phone calls now to see what the latest news is at United. Please call me if anything else unusual happens. It doesn't matter what time it is, I'm only 15 minutes away."

David walked her through to the lobby where Julia was waiting, checking her watch as they approached. They made their final farewells and David had turned to the elevator to make his way up to his room when he heard a voice call out behind him.

"David!" He turned to see Patrick, a broad grin plastered over his face, holding his arms out wide. He had a bottle of water in one hand, his room key in the other.

"Patrick!" David exclaimed, matching his enthusiasm. If only he knew, he thought as he embraced the young German. He could smell alcohol on him.

"Patrick, you've not been drinking have you – remember we have your medical tomorrow?"

Patrick laughed. "I knew you were going to say that. No, don't worry, I've been on the water all night – no way I'm going to mess this up. We can do our celebrating tomorrow. It was Monika," he gestured towards the young woman standing silently behind him, dressed head to toe in black. "She spilled some wine at dinner. It's fine, but I do need to change."

David gave a small nod of acknowledgement to Patrick's girlfriend. As he recalled, the two had been childhood sweethearts. David quietly hoped that the fame and glory of becoming a player in the best football league in the world wouldn't fracture their relationship as it had to so many others.

"And an early night, remember," David winked at Patrick, "I'll see you at breakfast?" He gave Patrick a slap on the back and began to head towards the elevators.

"Absolutely, David," Patrick called after him, "I can't wait to try my first Full English!"

David stepped into the elevator car and pressed the button for his floor. He turned to face Patrick, wearing a grin that he dropped the moment the doors closed.

31

Back in the hotel, Ander lay on his bed, shaken by his brother's news. His mind still wasn't quite letting the news sink in. However, one thing it had made him realise was that he now had to finish this deal without his brother's help.

He couldn't use his affair anymore. Couldn't destroy his family.

He checked his watch and hauled himself out of bed. He needed to get to the tenth floor lounge in time to meet the doctor.

He perched on his bed and waited, checking the stream of last-minute transfer news on his phone. To his delight, the Sun had reported exactly what he was waiting for.

For the first time today that he could remember, a genuine smile lit up Ander's face. No one could complain if Miller's player didn't pass the medical tomorrow. When he failed, the door was open for Merkel.

He glanced at his watch. It was almost 10pm. Ander left his room and scuttled down the corridor to the lounge where he informed the smartly dressed man at the desk that a guest would be joining him very soon.

Ander had seated himself in the far corner of the room in a large blue suede wingback chair. A well-matched retro table sat before him, sporting art and culture magazines and coffee-table books that looked like they hadn't been touched since they were placed there. Music played softly in the background – ambient chill-out tones gently accompanying the clink of glass and the quiet murmur of private conversations.

His thoughts turned to Joska as the guilt he felt for placing her in her awful situation grew. What kind of father was he? What kind of brother? What kind of man. Here he was sitting in the lounge of a boutique hotel when his only child was holed up in some dingy basement, the plaything of a group of people he had once wanted to be. If they had touched a hair on her head, there would be hell to pay. He would burn The Table to the ground even if it cost him his entire career. His life.

He was gazing into the middle distance, vaguely noticing the activity on the street below out of the top-floor window. Rain pelted the pavement as groups of men and women went about their nocturnal activity. Umbrellas floated and bobbed down the streets as people headed for the bars and clubs of the city, unperturbed by the weather. He was awoke from his daydream as he saw Rob Armstrong the head of Manchester United's medical team skulk into the lounge in the reflection of the plate glass.

He wore his cap so low that the brim nearly covered his eyebrows. No one could have seen his face on the way in.

Armstrong looked around cautiously. Football folk frequented the hotel, it was risky meeting here. It could cost Ander his deal, but also Armstrong's job. Finally, Armstrong sat down in front of Ander, his eyes glued to the entrance.

"Ander," he said, his voice barely above a whisper.

"Hi, Rob. Good to see you. How are things?"

Armstrong was a wily old man. He was thin and wiry, and his gaze constantly shifted around a room from under furrowed brow. He seemed to Ander to be wearing a permanent sneer, his lip curling up towards his squinting left eye. He had vast experience in the medical world and had begun his career as a junior doctor, hoping to make the lives of other people better. But the hours were long and the pay not worth it. When he had found the job at United, he had jumped at it.

"A lot of medicals these days. But all good so far," Armstrong answered noncommittally. He wasn't here to make friends, he was here to make money, and he wanted Ander to get to the point. He wasn't interested in Ander's networking bluster.

Ander picked up on the hint, "I need your help, Rob. This time it's very important and the reward is much higher than last time too."

The doctor sighed, "The German boy tomorrow morning?"

Ander nodded.

Armstrong twiddled his thumbs and stared blankly into space as he contemplated the situation.

"What's it worth?" He asked. The first time he'd taken a bung like this, Armstrong had felt a great shame wash over him, but here he was years later with two mortgages paid off, deposits paid on his kids houses, and an Aston Martin in the drive.

"How does a million sound?" Ander smiled, assuming this was guaranteed to win him over. "And half a mil each for the other two on your team."

"Convincing them won't be easy. There's a lot at risk for all of us. It's going to cost you three million. Two for me, given the extra work I've got to consider, and half for each of them," bartered Armstrong.

Ander was slightly irritated but maybe Armstrong had picked up on some of Ander's desperation.

"One and a half for you, five hundred grand for the other two. That's fair. I am not making any money out of this deal now. I'm losing money in fact, but I just need this deal."

"Done," said Armstrong, pleased that he'd manage to out-negotiate the hot-shot agent.

Ander breathed a deep sigh of relief, "Your money will arrive in the next week or so to the same bank account in Switzerland as before. Enjoy it!" he said, plastering a fake smile across his face.

"Pleasure doing business," said Armstrong as he stood from the seat. He took Ander's hand in a firm handshake, turned and left the lounge, pulling his cap back down over his eyes.

Ander watched the doctor leave as he gulped down the last of his drink. He felt relieved but was still not entirely assured. He couldn't get too far ahead of himself. He had to keep going. There was no space to relax until the dotted lines had been signed.

Ander's second drink had just arrived when another man blustered into the room in a crumpled suit. Clutching a battered brown leather bag by his side, he made way over to Ander's table.

He spoke to the waiter who had left Ander's table a moment ago and ordered himself a drink, pointing back over to the table. Ander presumed that John had charged the drink to his room.

John sat down hard into the chair opposite Ander, slouching immediately. He drummed his fingers on the leather arms of the chair, and Ander noticed his nails were bitten to the quick.

"Thanks for the news earlier today," said Ander as John rummaged through his bag, pulling out his notebook and flipping it open to a blank page. Ander laughed at his devotion to pen and paper – one of the most powerful tabloid sports journalists still did things old school. He didn't even use a Dictaphone.

"You don't have to thank me. Always there for you if need anything. You've looked after me very well all these years, amigo," smiled John, his Spanish accent straight out of a British sitcom.

It was exactly what Ander wanted to hear. He took the chance to push the journalist further.

"I need two bits of news to break tomorrow. In the morning, right after the medical, spread the news that he didn't pass because of his previous knee injury. An hour after that I need the public to hear that Markel has arrived in Manchester."

John was nodding, scribbling notes onto his pad in furious shorthand. His drink arrived and he took a sip without acknowledging the waiter who'd placed it in front of him.

"My name shouldn't be mentioned at all. You know how to do it," finished Ander.

"Leave it with me", answered John confidently, taking another slug of his lager.

"This is a small gift to begin with," said Ander, drawing a small envelope from his bag. John took the envelope and looked inside, rifling through the wad of notes that just about amounted to John's annual salary.

"The yacht is ready whenever you guys need a well-earned break. Now, let's have some drinks before tomorrow," said Ander joyfully.

This might just work after all.

32

Joska had lost track of the time, but the glimpses she had of the sky through the canopy above told her showed the sun to be over the mid-point.

She had been keeping away from the edge of the wood, walking downhill the whole time. It was slow-going, as she trudged through the undergrowth. The ground, untouched by the sun, was moist beneath her, the smell of the rotting leaves and mulch strong in her nostrils.

Joska was thirsty. The last thing she had drunk had been the bottle of water her captors had handed her. She sat down in the middle of a small clearing on an uprooted moss covered tree and opened her ears. She was hoping to hear the smallest of trickles, any sign of a water source close by.

Nothing.

Nothing but the faint chatter of birds as they went about their business in the treetops. Come close, stay away. Go, now. It couldn't be too far until she reached a town of some sort. People had lived in these hills for centuries. She would be safe there, whatever she found. She could call her father, he could sort out whatever it was that had put them into this situation. He had to.

The crack of a stick breaking shot through the woodland. Joska whipped her head around in the direction it had come from. Another crack, the sound of voices urging quiet.

Here they come, she thought, as she rose slowly, checking each step as she trod lightly, moving away from her resting place and heading downhill once more.

She didn't imagine the men following her were trained trackers, she wasn't worried about the traces of her footprints. But noise travelled huge distances out here, without the cacophony of modern life to drown it out. The crunch of leaves underfoot could bring them rushing towards her.

Joska crouched low and pushed off down the mountain.

After what felt like another hour or so, the forest had started to thin and give way to rough, rocky land. Cliff faces jutted out to her right as the mountains reached impossibly high into the sky.

The sun was low now as the sun made its inevitable way towards the horizon, and in the distance, Joska could make out the twinkling of streetlights.

She needed to move fast now. The voices of the men behind her had gotten quieter, she hadn't heard any movement for some time. Perhaps they'd given up for the day, thinking that the woods would take care of her.

She needed to move fast now, without the cover of the trees she was completely exposed. The ground was steeper here as the mountain dipped down into the town below. She spotted a rock in the distance and made off for it at a jog, keeping upright, treading on the front part of her foot, keeping her centre of gravity low to fight against the inertia of the slope.

She made it to the first rock and took a moment to catch her breath and find her next waypoint. She checked the treeline behind her where she'd just left. It was hard to make anything out in the twilight that was quickly descending over the mountainside, but she couldn't make out any sign of the people who were following her.

Feeling confident, she moved off again for the next piece of cover. The ground here was rockier, less stable, and as she placed her foot down on a sturdy rock it moved underneath her. She was thrown off balance and landed hard on her hip. Joska sucked in air as the pain shot through her but avoided crying out. She placed both hands on the ground and hoisted herself up again. Moving forward again, she winced as the pain in her hip pinched. Nothing was broken, but there'd be a hell of a bruise in the morning.

Morning. She would make it to the next morning. Battered, bruised, but alive.

A wind blew across the face of the mountain and reminded her of how exposed she was. Up here, the air was cooler and with the sun now almost set she would have to find a warm place to spend the night. Some more clothes.

The town below her became more distinct as more streetlights and windows lit up. Car headlights illuminated the winding single-track roads then wound through the place.

A row of houses backed onto the mountains, a low brick wall doing its best to separate them from the silent megaliths. As she drew closer, Joska could see large rocks piled up against the back wall and it became clear the wall served a significant purpose. These hills were alive, ever-changing, and the danger of rockslides was ever present.

Eventually, Joska reached the edge of town and with one last look behind her, checking the coast was clear, she walked out onto the street hoping to find someone who could help her.

33

After settling into his rooms, David had called Patrick to go through the briefing for deadline day. Tomorrow was a huge day for both of them.

The medical would be first thing in the morning, and the signing was planned after lunch, with press and media interviews taking place afterwards. Patrick would then stay in the hotel until he found a place to live, which David promised to help him with.

"Thank you, David," said Patrick, "For everything you've done for me and my family."

"I haven't done anything," replied David, "Your success on the pitch is why we are here today. I am proud of you. You've fought back after your injury and done a fantastic job."

"You know David, me and my family love the way you are. Always humble and down to earth," he said smiling.

"Thanks Patrick. You should go to bed now. You have to rest before tomorrow. We will want to celebrate in the afternoon," said David with a smirk.

David sat back on the bed and flicked onto the sports news on his laptop.

His heart sank a little. I knew they would write about it.

He was reading the Sun's story about Patrick's medical past and the concern about his last injury. The news was already all over the tabloid papers and flooding social media. It was even trending on Twitter.

He hoped that Patrick didn't read it before he went to bed. He didn't need a last-minute worry.

A notification popped up on his screen. A message from Annabel.

On way back to hotel. Starving. Room service?

David smiled as the worries from the day washed away.

Reception had called announcing Annabel's arrival. The person on the desk had sounded sceptical. It wasn't unusual for single male guests to receive female visitors at the inner city hotel.

"It's fine, please send her up – and you can charge the room as a double if that makes things easier," he hoped he wasn't being too presumptuous, "Can I check, are the kitchens still open? My friend will be starving – we've both had a long day."

"Yes, sir – just let us know what you'd like to order. I'll send your guest up now."

A few minutes later, there was a light knock at the door. David pulled it open, trying not to look to eager. Annabel looked amazing, David had to stop himself from gawping.

"Come in," he said, barely managing to get the words out.

Annabel smiled and leaned in planting a small kiss on David's cheek. Had she lingered there slightly? David was exerting every ounce of willpower he had. Take it slow. Be normal.

Annabel flopped down onto the bed, arms and legs splayed out and sighed deeply.

"Where's this room service then?" she asked, rolling over to the bedside table and pulling the menu out of the drawer. "Are you having anything? Do they have chips?"

David smiled.

"I reckon. Burger and chips twice? Full fat Coke?"

He was picking up the receiver on the room phone.

"I wonder who spread this news about Patrick's injury?" Annabel asked as David waited for reception to pick up. "I know he has a fair few journalists in his phonebook and on his payroll," replied Annabel.

"Journalists?" scoffed David, briefly forgetting what he'd seen downstairs. "You can't call these people making tabloid news journalists."

They both laughed.

"He's not going to make it easy, is he?" said David. "I wonder what his next play will be?"

After placing the order, David joined Annabel on the bed, propping up pillows against the headboard and switching on the television that was strapped to the wall. He flicked idly through the channels before landing on a movie. He'd seen it before, but Annabel hadn't. The two of them leaned back against the bed and watched in silence.

"This is nice," Annabel said after a while.

"Yeah," replied David. It was; whilst he could barely take his eyes off of her, it felt completely natural to be lying with her, half-watching a film.

"Where are my chips, though?" David had completely forgotten the food order. He rolled over and picked up the phone, dialling for reception. There was no answer.

"I'll just nip down and see what's going on," he said, and grabbed his key card.

As the elevator doors opened into the lobby, David's attention was immediately drawn to the two men who were checking in at the desk. Both were tall and wore smart, designer suits. He overheard them talking to the woman at the reception desk and noticed their heavy Spanish accents.

They gave their luggage to the bellman and headed straight to the hotel bar on the other side of the lobby. David instinctively turned his face away as they walked past. He made his way to the desk, ensuring he kept his back to the bar and enquired about their meals.

"Apologies, sir. I'll check in with the kitchen and have them sent up as soon as they're ready."

He turned sharply, and headed back over to the elevator, grateful that he had come down in his socks. He was completely silent as he made his way across the marble floor.

He pressed the button to call the elevator and tried to act nonchalant, pulling out his phone to check his emails. But he couldn't focus on the screen. The elevator dinged its arrival and the doors opened. He walked in and pressed for the ninth floor.

The doors were almost close when a tattooed hand shot into the gap and pulled it open. The two men he'd seen checking in scuttled inside to join him. Neither pressed any button on the control panel.

Perhaps they're on my floor, thought David. But he knew that was wishful thinking. Something felt strange. Something about the way the men refused to turn around and acknowledge his presence. The two men faced away from him towards the doors of the elevator.

David had no choice but to stare at the backs of their heads. There it was. David stomach dropped.

The same tattoo that he had seen earlier today on the train. The snake.

He noticed one of the men scanning the corners of the lift car. Looking for cameras, David thought. There wasn't one. His palms began to feel clammy as his heartbeat accelerated. He tried to bring it back under control, breathing slowly, deliberately. He needed to be calm for whatever was about to happen.

Without turning to him, one of the men spoke. "We'll follow you to your room. We would like to talk about our friends on the train. Do not worry, we are not here to hurt you."

David was terrified. He didn't believe that for a second. He wasn't built for fighting, and he was leading these brutes back to his room. Back to Annabel. He tried to survey his options. He could run. Get to the front desk. Call the police. But then they'd be alone with Annabel. His knees were weak as he resigned himself to his fate.

The elevator stopped and the doors opened. The three men exited together. The corridor was empty, the bright wall lamps illuminating the scene in an unnatural light – it was dark outside, but the light here felt like daylight.

The men followed David, constantly scanning for cameras. There was a camera halfway along the corridor, and the men ducked their heads, staying a few paces behind David so as not to arouse suspicion.

They reached the door to David's room, and he hesitated. He could feel their presence directly behind him.

"No funny business," it was the other man talking now, his voice a nasal whine.

David's hand rose to knock.

"Annabel," he spoke through the door, "It's me. Can you let me in, I've left my key card in there."

They heard the sound of someone heaving themselves out of bed and padding over to the door. There was a brief scratching around the wall and the click of a light switch. A thin section of light crept out from beneath the door.

The handle clunked but stayed closed.

"I've just latched it. Sorry, busting for the loo since I stood up," Annabel called through the door.

David placed his hand on the handle and turned it gingerly, opening the door by a fraction. The men pushed him forwards and all three moved into the room.

In a split second David heard the second man grunt and stumble forwards. David turned to see Annabel brandishing a lamp and ducked fast to avoid her second swing which she aimed directly at the head of the other thug.

"Run!" she yelled, bringing the lamp down on top of the man's head again.

David yanked open the door and kicked at the nasal-voiced man, who hadn't gone fully down. The man scrambled forward, caught up in a tangle of limbs with his partner.

David grabbed Annabel, who was kicking at the hands of the larger man as he clutched at her ankles. David stamped at the man's hand, hearing a crunch as he smashed his fingers into the ground. The man let out an excruciating wail and dropped Annabel's ankle.

David and Annabel ran through the door, slamming it shut behind them. They sprinted for the escalator, but then Annabel shouted to David.

"No, the stairs!" and bolted through a door off to the side.

David took the stairs two at a time, desperately trying to keep pace with Annabel who was flying full tilt.

"Get to the garage. I gave Malik the night off," she pulled her keys from her bag. "Come on, Davey, get moving."

She's enjoying this, thought David as he noticed the grin beaming across her face.

They reached the basement level and Annabel held the door for David, her chest heaving as she got her breath back. They slowed their pace to a fast walk and crossed the parking lot to where Annabel's blacked out Mercedes waited.

David climbed into the passenger seat as Annabel started the ignition.

"Right, where to?" he asked her.

"I know just the place," she said, and reversed the car, turning the wheel hard. As she put the car into gear, the tyres squealed against the floor of the parking lot and Annabel and David fled into the city night.

As they sped through the Manchester streets, Annabel had her eyes glued to her mirrors. There was no doubt the men would give chase. They needed to get as much distance between them as quickly as possible.

She glanced at David. "What are you doing?"

"I'm thinking," he replied, his fingers swiping over his phone screen seemingly randomly as far as Annabel could see.

"You need to try to stop panicking," she said, affecting as calm a voice as possible. The adrenaline of the chase was wearing off and she could feel herself relaxing now. "We both need to be on our a-game if we're going to get out of this unscathed."

"I need to phone the boys, see if they've got everything sorted for tomorrow," David said eventually.

"It's late…" Annabel checked the clock on the dash.

"They'll be awake. No doubt they completely ignored me and they're out on the lash. Pre-celebrations, William usually calls it." Annabel let out a small laugh and David felt a lightness descend on him.

He found Jose's number and called. After several seconds, the call diverted to his answer phone. He tried again. It wasn't wort trying William – even when he had his phone on him, it was usually out of battery.

There was still no answer.

"Huh, maybe they did get an early night after all – it keeps going through to voicemail," he said, though he felt a slight panic rising again.

"Look, let's just get to mine and lay low – they can't chase us all around town. It's not some kind of gangster movie. Once the deal is done, the threat is over. We just need to get through to tomorrow's meetings. They'll never reach you at the training grou—"

She was cut short by the trill of David's phone. The caller ID showed it was William.

"William, mate – you'll never believe what's happening here. Everything's going completely crazy. I was just calling Jose to check that everyth—"

It was David's turn to get cut off this time.

"David. I didn't want to call you as I knew you'd start to worry."

David's brow furrowed with concern. William sounded tired, a little shellshocked.

"It's Jose, David. He's in the hospital – they messed him up pretty bad." His voice quavered as he relayed the news to David.

"Wh—what do you mean? Who got him?"

"The Basques, man. The guys who've been following you all this time. They must have followed Jose back to the office. They've kicked seven shades out of him."

"How do you know it's them?" David couldn't quite believe what he was hearing.

"They left a note," Williams tone was sombre, "Addressed to you. Says 'She's next.'"

David turned to Annabel. She'd heard everything over the speakerphone. Her face was ashen.

"William, I've got to go. Is Jose okay?"

"Aye, he'll live. I'm with him now – they don't make it comfortable, visiting in these hospitals."

David made his goodbyes and hung up the phone.

"Well," he said, "That's your place off the cards. Where to?"

Annabel thought for a moment. David watched her face as she crossed off a mental checklist of safehouses. When you broke the sorts of stories Annabel did, you always had a backup.

"I have an idea," she said, taking a sharp left away from the centre of town.

34

In the past, the pre-signing medical had been more of a formality and never took too long. Nowadays, clubs wanted to ensure that the millions of pounds they were spending on players was getting them an elite, perfectly functioning athlete. The process had become far more complex and rigorous.

"How was your ACL surgery?" asked Armstrong, in the medical centre of Manchester United's revolutionary training ground. "And remind me which doctor did the operation?"

"Dr Markus Brenz," said Patrick proudly, "A top class knee specialist from Innsbruck. I had a very speedy recovery and have had no problem since then."

"Do you ever have pain or stiffness around the knee?" asked Armstrong.

"No, not at all. It feels very good," answered Patrick, clearly he hadn't made himself clear that there had been no problem since the operation.

Armstrong continued to prod and probe his wiry fingers around Patrick's kneecap.

"Your knee stability doesn't seem to be one-hundred-percent but that's no big issue and is very common after an ACL surgery. It feels like there is a small patch of tenderness and inflammation around the patella tendon. This usually occurs after an ACL surgery with a patella tendon graft. The procedure involves having the middle third portion of the tendon removed to make the new graft. Do you feel any pain if I press with my finger into this side of your knee?" asked Armstrong as he plunged his finger into Patrick's leg.

"No, not at all. It feels normal," replied Patrick, holding back his grimace. It wasn't that his history was causing him problems it was just the sheer force it was being prodded with. It was as if Armstrong was trying to cause pain so that Patrick would say yes.

Armstrong seemed disappointed, sighing as he nodded slowly and removed his gloves.

"Well done, we will send you over to the hospital to get a cardiac ECG screening and some other standard tests to check your urine and all that. They'll be doing some scans around your knee and some other areas. I will advise Dr Sampson to double check that knee and give me a report as well. My colleague will be with you and assist you throughout the morning."

"Thanks Doctor," said Patrick, begrudgingly. He shrugged his shoulders. There was nothing he could do. This was the worst part of the day but then this afternoon it would all be worth it when he signed as a United player.

When everyone had left his examination room, Armstrong took the phone and called his friend at the hospital.

"Morning, Tom. The boy will be in soon, you know what to do, right?" asked Armstrong quietly.

"Don't worry," Dr Tom Sampson reassured him, "Everything will be done as discussed yesterday. Can't wait to go on that holiday, mate."

"Perfect, I'll be here and waiting for your report," said Armstrong.

35

Annabel and David had arrived at Malik's house at around two in the morning. Annable drop called him from the car and he had called straight back. Minutes later, they had the keys to Malik's family saloon and were backing out of his driveway with Annabel's car parked on the street.

They had reached Julia's house around an hour later. She had been waiting for them. Malik had called ahead. David marvelled at the well-oiled machine these three had created.

Julia had taken them through the house and out through the back door. David looked around on his way through and noted how strange it was that there didn't seem to be anything in the house at all. No pictures on the wall, which wasn't hugely strange, but as he peered into what would traditionally have been the front room there was nothing. No sofa, no coffee table. Just a lamp with no shade, the bare bulb casting its harsh light throughout the room, and a sleeping bag rolled out onto a camp bed. A laptop sat atop everything, alongside a notepad and several sets of paper strewn across the floor.

From the back garden, there was a large metal door in the side of what David discerned to be the garage. The door had no handle, instead Julia inserted a key with a cross bar on it which acted as a handle and enabled her to pull the door open. They walked through and David's eyes widened in surprise. He heard Annabel laugh through her nose.

They were now standing in some sort of bunker. Metal racking lined the walls, filled with tinned and jarred produce. An air ventilation system stood dormant at the back of the room, its aluminium ventilation pipes snaking up towards the roof.

David spun around, taking note of the clothes storage, the tools hanging from the walls, and the reams of toilet paper stacked high.

He turned to Annabel, not quite understanding what to make of it all. She shrugged.

"You'll be safe here," Julia interrupted, rolling out sleeping mats and taking down two stuff-packed sleeping bags.

"I'll be next door, but if you need me, you can press this button," she pointed to an intercom by the door. "Try to get some sleep. Do you need anything?"

"I think we've got everything we need right here," said David, and he couldn't help but laugh. Annabel joined in, and Julia backed out of the room, leaving them to it.

***

The next morning, David felt like he'd barely closed his eyes. He had crawled over to the workbench Julia had set up, still in his sleeping bag, and had found a place to charge his phone. He had been checking the news, looking for any information about the guys who had attacked them. There was nothing, which told David precisely what he didn't want to hear. They were still out there, which meant they'd be looking for them.

He heard the rustle of polyester from the other side of the room.

"Did you manage to get some sleep?" he asked Annabel.

"Hm, some," Annabel had brought herself up to sitting, her hair was standing at the back as she blinked away the sleep in her eyes. "What time is it?"

If this was any other circumstance, David thought, the thought of waking up next to Annabel would be something to celebrate.

"A little after six."

"So, what's the plan?" Annabel was extracting herself from her cocoon, still wearing the clothes she had on last night.

"Well, I have to be at the ground for half nine. I don't think there's much we can do in the meantime. Except maybe get some breakfast. I'm starving after we skipped dinner last night!" David said.

"Great thinking," Annabel agreed, "Let me buzz Julia." She pressed the button the intercom that Julia had showed them. A few seconds later, the steel door clunked as the complex internal locking mechanism disengaged and the door swung open.

Julia was holding two mugs of coffee and handed one to Annabel.

"Morning, campers," she smiled and passed the second cup to David. "So, are you going to tell me what happened last night or am I going to have to piece it together myself?"

The three of them walked through to the main house and into the kitchen, where Julia began to cook eggs over the stove. David and Annabel filled her in on what had gone on in the hotel.

"I mean, I know Ander's a menace, but this seems pretty extreme," Julia got two plates down from a cupboard and slid breakfast onto them, "I don't know… it feels like maybe this is getting away from him. Like the guys he was working with have turned on him."

Annabel agreed, "I mean, it's possible. He's an arsehole, I have no doubt he escalated things with poor Jose…" she paused, "Have you heard anything more?"

"I've been messaging William. Seems like it was a bit touch and go – they were worried about a brain bleed, but I think he's out of the woods now. In a lot of pain, a few broken ribs, but thankfully nothing life-threatening," David still couldn't quite believe what had happened. He had felt guilty when he'd woken up, for putting his friends in such an awful position – and fearful for any further danger he might put them, or his family, in. But it wasn't his fault, he told himself, it was all on Anaia. The faster David could get his deal signed, the sooner this would all be over, and everyone would be safe.

The faster he could help Annabel and Julia break their story and bring Ander, and The Table, to justice.

"I'm glad to hear it," Annabel continued, "But yeah, it feels like last night was one step too far for Ander. Those guys were really going to hurt us, and there's no way they couldn't be linked back to him now. Why else would we be a target? Anaia doesn't make rash moves."

"Well, you'll be safe here 'til you're needed," Julia said, "There are towels in the bathroom. Get yourselves cleaned up. David, give me your clothes, I'll wash them – you can't go to your meeting looking like that."

David looked down at his crumpled shirt and took the hint. He went through to the bathroom and turned on the water to full. The coffee had begun the long process of bringing him back to life, the shower would take him one step closer to feeling human again.

Then he just had to figure out where to find some shoes.

36

Joska woke to the dawn light breaking through a gap in the wooden boards. She had crept into a back garden under the cover of darkness and taken shelter in a woodshed.

It was a dirt floor, but she had found a pile of hessian sacks and laid them out to stop the cold of the earth seeping through into her bones.

Joska calculated that she must have managed a few hours' sleep. She didn't feel quite as refreshed as she would have done had she been waking up at her father's house, wrapped in cotton sheets, but it had taken the edge off of her exhaustion.

Her main priority now, though, was water. And food. She had gone most of the day without a drink yesterday, and the effort of making her way through the woods and down the side of the mountain had been tough going.

She would have to walk into town and try her luck at a café. Hopefully the owner would take pity on her. God knew she looked the part.

Joska hoisted herself up to standing, her bones creaking as she unfolded. She cracked open the door to the shed and scanned the area, trying to make out which direction would take her to the centre of town.

It was still early morning and most of the streets were empty. Joska picked her way down a narrow street, keeping close to the buildings, making herself as small as possible. She still couldn't be sure she had lost her pursuers. For all she knew, this could be the only town for miles. It wouldn't take much effort for them to camp out and wait for her to show herself.

Joska froze. The sound of footsteps gaining on her rapidly echoed off of the cobblestones behind her. She frantically scanned her surroundings, looking for a place to hide but found nothing. As the footsteps got louder, she felt frozen to the spot. She tried to regain control, to get past the freeze instinct and go into fight or flight mode.

She noticed a box outside the closest house, filled with empty bottles for recycling and bent to pick up the heaviest one.

Joska gripped the neck of the bottle tight and turned to face her pursuer. Heart racing, hands sweating she rocked back onto her back foot. She knew she didn't have the energy for flight. It would have to be fight.

As she turned, she saw the man's eyes widen in alarm as he kept pace and feinted around her right side without dropping his pace.

Joska dropped the bottle, the smash of the glass cracking through the early morning silence and watched the early-morning jogger speed up into the distance, occasionally glancing behind him to check he wasn't being followed by the crazy bottle-wielding girl. She couldn't help but laugh, which she was sure only helped the runner pick up the pace more. Perhaps she'd inspire him to a personal best this morning.

Joska swept the glass to the side of the path with her foot and carried on.

As she emerged into the central plaza, more signs of life began to show. Tiny cars that she couldn't believe managed to navigate the steep mountain terrain putted around the narrow streets, window shutters opened, letting the fresh mountain air blow through apartments.

A group of young boys in football kits jostled one another as they made their way up the road, on their way to early morning practise before school.

Joska headed towards a café on the other side of the square. Some tables and cheap garden furniture were situated outside, and the place was already busy with people drinking their morning coffees. A couple of tourists wearing expensive hiking clothes occupied two tables closest to the square.

She approached the man, a tall, handsome blonde guy wearing Oakley wraparound shades, a well-worn baseball cap emblazoned with the name of some sports team pulled down over his head.

"Excuse me, sir," Joska said, her voice meek as it croaked out of her parched throat.

"I'm sorry," he replied, barely looking up at her, "*No habla Espanol.* No money. No money." He rubbed his finger and thumb together, shaking his head.

"Cole, don't be such an asshole," a female voice off to the right said, and Joska turned to see a young woman about the same age as she was, perched atop her giant rucksack. Joska couldn't believe she planned to carry the thing up the mountain.

"Here, honey, take this," said the young woman, fishing into a pack cinched around her waist. She handed Joska a twenty Euro note and flashed her a genuine smile.

Joska was a little shellshocked. She must look awful. But then what did she expect. She hadn't showered for days, had barely drunk let alone eaten. And last night she'd slept in a shed. She stared at the note in the woman's outstretched hand. She had no other option, really. She felt a pang of guilt as she took the money.

"Thank you," she said, and vowed to pay the good deed forward.

"No problem, sweetie. In fact… Cole, give me your wallet," without waiting for him to respond, she dug into the pocket of his coat and pulled out a cloth wallet. She tore open the Velcro strap.

"Hey!" Cole made a half-hearted attempt to snatch it back, but the woman held it out of reach.

"Here, take this as well." And she handed Joska another twenty Euro note, "Get yourself some warm clothes, it's cold up here."

Joska thanked her again, and thanked Cole, and moved off to a table nearer to the café. As she sat, she saw Cole take his wallet back from the woman, shaking his head. The two began to gather up their things and as they went to leave, the woman turned and waved. "Stay safe, honey."

Joska waved back.

After a few minutes, a gruff moustachioed man emerged from the café to take her order.

"What's good?" Joska asked, feeling him looking down on her as he took in her mud-caked legs, her birds nest hair.

"Everything," he answered. Clearly a place that prided itself on customer service.

"I'll have a café con leche, please. Do you have churros?" The man nodded. "Churros, then – and Pan con Tomate. And water. A big jug, please." The man took down her order in silence and went off to prepare the food.

A few minutes later, he had returned, order in hand and gracelessly placed it down in front of Joska. It had barely hit the table before she started filling herself with delicious fresh bread soaked in olive oil, wafer thin slices of jambon folded on top.

She filled a glass and took a long slug of water. It was ice cold and she felt it course through her body, instantly reviving her.

As she ate, a man came to sit at the table next to her. He placed his order and pulled out a newspaper, turning to the back sports pages. He was handsome, tall and slim, his blue eyes made all the brighter by his otherwise dark complexion. When he spoke, it made Joska jump.

"Barcelona hasn't been the same without Messi," he announced, clearly trying to grab her attention. She couldn't care less about football, she got enough of that when she spoke to her dad. She'd never been interested in following in his footsteps, much to Ander's dismay.

"Sure," she responded, not committing to an opinion, out of politeness. Why did men always feel the need to talk to women in public places. A man could go to any bar, club or café in the world and be completely ignored if they wanted. Men seemed to think a woman alone in one of these places was just waiting for a man to come over and talk to her.

"Hungry?" he asked, eyebrows raised, as he surveyed the remains of Joska's breakfast. The morning sun was fully up in the sky now, and it warmed the patio where they sat.

"Been a long time since I last ate, honestly," she said, a little embarrassed that he'd noticed.

"Trouble?" he asked.

"Something like that..."

"Anything I can help with?" he kept on pressing.

"I doubt it," Joska was trying, and failing, to shut down the conversation but the man kept trying to advance.

"Do you need a lift anywhere? You're not from around here, I don't think?"

Joska paused to consider her options. The guy looked harmless enough. Clearly, he'd seen what a state she was in, and was just being a good citizen. She had accepted help from the American woman before, there was no reason she had not to trust this man now. People were good. These people were good.

"Actually, yes," she said, finally, "I'm trying to get down the mountain. I need to get back to San Sebastian where my dad lives." The man frowned, the ride to San Sebastian was a long way, especially for a round trip. "I wouldn't expect you to take me all the way," Joska swiftly added, "I've money for cab fare, but I just know no one will come to pick me up all the way out here."

The man chewed on the idea for a few moments. He drank the remnants of his coffee.

"I can take you as far as Tolosa," he said, folding his paper under his arm. He stood up, placing enough money on the table to cover both their bills. "Come on, let's go, before I change my mind."

Joska jumped up, beaming.

"Thank you! You're a complete life saver." You don't know how literally I mean that, she thought.

They crossed back over the square, heading towards an SUV. The headlights lit up as the man disengaged the central locking. She paused for a moment, her hand resting on the door handle, as she considered what she was doing.

"Something wrong?" the man asked, sensing her hesitance.

"No," Joska said, opening up the car door and climbing inside. The car was a luxury model. The interior was upholstered in leather, with a walnut dash, and had that 'new car' smell. As the man started the engine, she felt the seat warm beneath her.

"Okay, let's go," said the man, putting the car into reverse. He held out his hand, "I'm Micah, by the way."

"Joska," she said, taking his hand firmly and shaking it.

Joska settled into the car, making sure to plug in her seatbelt. She rested her head on the passenger side window as Micah navigated his way through the winding streets.

She watched the morning sun light up the mountainside and smiled as she began to relax. She was on her way to safety, away from whoever it was who had taken her. She would call her dad and he would know what to do.

"Hey, Micah," Joska said, as they passed a road sign, "That sign said Tolosa was the other direction."

Micah shifted in his seat but said nothing. Joska felt the car accelerate beneath her.

"Micah?" she asked again, but still he maintained his silence. The car hugged the road, but Joska heard the faintest squeal of rubber as he took several long bending corners too fast.

"Let me out," she demanded. She pulled helplessly against the door handle, but it didn't budge.

"Let me out, you fucking animal," she screamed at him, throwing her fists towards him.

Micah brushed off her attack, and continued driving, taking Joska further back up the mountain.

37

"Good morning. David Smith. I have a meeting with Aitor Gaizka," said David to the guard.

"Good morning, sir," the woman replied, opening the cab door and motioning towards the gates. David surveyed the security outside the front of the Manchester United AON training ground and was grateful to see they had it on complete lockdown. No one got near the place without ID checks and facing the brunt of several serious looking security staff.

He had felt nervous leaving Annabel, but she and Julia had assured him she'd be safe.

"This isn't my first rodeo," Annabel had said. David smiled at the memory.

David paid the cab driver in cash and walked inside the training ground. It had been three months since the first time he had come here to meet the management and Aitor Gaizka to talk about a potential move for Patrick to Manchester United.

Since that day he had kept in touch with Aitor on a regular basis. After a seemingly endless string of emails and phone calls, an agreement was made upon a final offer.

The proposal was a lifechanging one for Patrick as well as for David. Once this deal was completed, Patrick would be earning £100,000 a week for five years, with a whole host of annual bonuses and such. Things would never be the same again.

This deal would also change his life. He could finally pay off his university debt, help his dad out with his financial problems and still have money left over to move into a nicer apartment back in London.

His goal was to move to further north, preferably to Highgate or Hampstead even though he would miss his neighbour, George.

When he'd received the offer, he couldn't stop his mind from dreaming. Towards the top of his priorities lay his desire to have his own luxury, tailored suits. But nothing would ever come above the most important motivation to finish this deal. His mother.

Last week he had been in Germany and visited her grave. Through the tears, which would never stop, no matter how many times he visited, he had promised her that he would finish this deal and would take care of her family. It was what he had promised when she was sick in hospital and was a promise he would never break.

He arrived at the main building of the complex and walked inside. Victoria was waiting for him.

"Good morning, Mr. Smith, pleasure to see you again," said Victoria with a wide front-of-house smile. "Aitor's just in a meeting with the management right now but he'll be with you as soon as he is finished. I'll let him know that you've arrived. Can I offer you a drink in the meantime?" asked Victoria. It was clear to David why Victoria had been in the job so long. She was approachable, friendly and just the right amount of deferential. She made new arrivals feel comfortable, and well informed.

"I wouldn't say no to a good coffee," replied David.

"I'll assume you're a man who would prefer a properly brewed coffee rather than from a machine?" asked Victoria.

"That would be fantastic!" replied David, encouraged by her friendliness. He wondered whether she'd noticed the redness he'd not been able to get rid of in the shower. He was running on adrenaline and caffeine after getting no sleep the night before. "And maybe two matchsticks to hold my eyelids open? Didn't get much sleep last night," he decided to confront the matter head on.

Victoria let out a polite laugh. "No problem at all. I wouldn't have slept a wink last night either. Exciting times! Please have a seat and make yourself comfortable. I'll bring it to you as soon as it's ready."

David sunk into one of the luxurious seats in the lobby area and fixed his eyes on one of the two big TV screens showing the Sky Sports news coverage of deadline day. Two men and a woman were discussing the new Arsenal signing that had been completed in the last few hours – a star player, it had upset the football world somewhat. If nothing else, the player had signed up to be booed every time his new team visited the Emirates.

Victoria returned a while later with the coffee. David had turned away from the television and was flicking through the morning papers strewn on the table in front of him.

"Here you go, David. I brought you milk and sugar just in case" she said, placing everything down in front of him.

"Thanks Victoria," David said, reaching forward for the steaming mug of coffee "Not for me, though. I take my coffee straight — strong and black."

He felt a brief moment of bliss as he reclined in the seat and sipped gently on his hot, delicious coffee.

The Sky Sports tune rung in his ears. He turned his head to face at the screen. The sound was off, but he read the subtitles across the bottom of the screen.

Manchester United is preparing to withdraw their offer for the young German attacker, Patrick Maier, because of his medical difficulties and history. Instead, it is reported that they are about to sign their other young Spanish target from Bilbao, Markel. He was spotted landing in Manchester this morning and will have his own medical later today.

One of the announcers shook their head in shock as he spoke.

"Victoria," David said, "Can you turn this up?"

Victoria fished around in her desk drawer for the remote and turned the volume up a few notches.

"So," said one of the pundits, "Looks like the Basque mafia at United strikes again. Rachel, despite all the speculation into the collapse of their relationship, it looks like the manager-agent Basque pair of Ander and Marco look like they're going to bring another player to United after all! I actually like the German player a lot. But if his knee problems are going to be an issue at United then the sensible thing to do is to go for Markel instead?" his voice rose at the end of the sentence, turning his statement into a question.

The woman, Rachel, agreed.

"There's no denying that there is a strong correlation between the players United sign and the brothers. Marco Anaia certainly has a massive influence at that club, and not just as the manager. Roy?"

The third man, the eldest of the three chimed in now. He was more openly negative than the other two, his years of experience talking about the game giving him a world weariness.

"Well, I don't think there's much argument in the fact that Ander Anaia's players have never been the best. More often than not they end up loaned out within a few years, if they even get a first team run out. It doesn't take a genius to connect the dots. I can't think of many other reasons why Ander Anaia consistently manages to place mediocre players at one of the biggest clubs in the world."

"Because the coach's brother is the most powerful agent in this club!" a harsh voice boomed next to David.

David turned to see Ander Anaia standing next to him, coat slung across his arm, espresso cup in hand. He brought the cup to his lips and drained it in one hit.

"You must be surprised to see me here, boy?" sneered Ander, emphasising the "boy." "I thought we might see each other at some point."

David was shocked at his sudden arrival but wasn't going to let it show. He didn't want Ander to know that the events of the last few days had affected him.

"I would be far more surprised if I didn't see you here. The way this club is run sometimes, I'm surprised you haven't got your own office," David fired back quickly, "So it's no surprise at all to see you skulking around here, sticking your tentacles into everyone's business."

Ander huffed, "I warned you so many times that it would be smarter to abandon all your talks with this club. You didn't listen. Who do you think you are?"

"You are not someone I respect," David responded, working hard to keep his tone measured, "So why would I listen to you?"

Ander looked surprised. David had even surprised himself. Since when did he have the courage to talk to anybody like that, let alone one of the most influential people at Manchester United?

"So, who do you think you are Ander? And all this for a seat at The Table."

The look on Ander's face told David he had gone too far, but he didn't care. He wanted Ander scared. Wanted to give him even an ounce of what he and Annabel had been put through. He wanted to make to ensure Ander wouldn't forget him or mess with his business again.

Ander's face glowed red. David had hit him right where it hurt the most. It was Ander's turn now to keep his emotions in check. The area where they were stood was very exposed, with people going about their business all around. The last thing Ander needed now was footage leaking of him losing his cool. It would tank his deal. It would mean that he had failed The Table. And they still had Joska.

He pulled himself together and leaned in towards David. He grabbed his shoulder firmly as he whispered in his ear, "It seems that your boy has a very big knee problem. This club doesn't like signing players with a bad medical report. There's no going back from a Sky Sports headline like that. I guess they'll have to sign my boy instead."

Ander wore a cruel grin as he leaned back into his chair.

"This is ridiculous," exclaimed David despairingly, "He is one-hundred-percent ready to play. He fully recovered from his knee injury a year ago. I'd watch your next move, Ander – your dirty tricks have all failed, and now all you have left is an honest to goodness competition. Patrick is twice the athlete Markel is. You know it, I know it – your brother knows it."

The smirk was wiped off of Ander's face at once, and he began breathing in and out, forcing himself to take control of his emotions. David had no idea what he was saying. No idea of the risks Ander had taken.

David held his stare but was distracted as he heard Patrick's name announced again on the television behind him.

The news on the screen now took a second to land before crushing them both. Footage of Danny Mixton, a Burnley winger, was playing accompanied by headlines announcing him as first choice for the position, ahead of both David and Ander's players.

Ander and David stood in silence, staring at the screen in disbelief.

"Seems like we both have a big problem now," David said, forcing a smile as he turned to his opponent, taking some solace in the look on Ander's face. He seemed utterly crushed. His legs seemed to buckle, and he sat down on the arm of the chair that David had previously occupied.

Ander's eyes were still glued to the screen. Tears filled his eyes. Ander looked to a screen showing BBC News and a story caught his eye.

Train Execution Terror Link: Two men found dead on train linked to Basque separatist group, ETA. Two more members arrested in Manchester city centre hotel.

"Joska," David heard him whisper, "This cannot be happening. I won't let it." He was staring into the middle distance now, his cheeks streaked with tears. He wiped them away, shook himself and stood up.

He drew his phone from his pocket and exited the building without sparing a glance for David or Victoria, who looked on, bemused.

“Mr. Anaia,” the voice on the other end of the line drawled. "I'm not liking what I'm seeing on the television set.”

“This has to end, Farmington,” Ander was stopping himself from yelling down the phone. “Let my daughter go, or the deal is off.”

There was silence on the line, and then Ander heard Jack Farmington begin to laugh. Softly at first, but it gathered power and became a hearty laugh. Ander could do nothing but stand and listen, waiting for him to stop.

“Mr. Anaia,” Farmington eventually brought his laughter under control, “We at The Table had been previously very encouraged by your understanding of how we conduct our business. In fact, a few of us here saw you as a natural fit. But there seems to be something you have not understood in all this. Your daughter is our property now. The success of this deal is not just how you gain your place amongst my esteemed colleagues. It is how you buy her back.” Ander could hear the smile on his face.

“That wasn’t the deal,” Ander was losing control.

“It was always the deal,” Farmington had lost his sense of humour, “If you were so naïve that you didn’t think we’d take some collateral to ensure everything went off without a hitch, that’s on you.”

“Collateral? She’s my daughter. She’s a human being,” Ander was getting more frantic as the conversation went on. He had stopped marching back and forth now and was stood stock still, the phone pressed against his ear. He felt bile rise in his stomach, the caffeine working in tandem with the adrenaline to make his heart pound so that it felt like it would burst through his chest.

"And what about all of the other 'human beings' you invited to your soirees, Anaia? Where do you think all of those girls came from? As I said, there's a lot of money riding on your boy landing at United. If it doesn't work out, we'll keep the girl. She can help us earn it back."

Ander couldn't believe what he was hearing. He had been so stupid. He had been outplayed. He hung up the phone and sank to his knees.

It took Ander several minutes to regain his composure, and he was thankful that the parking lot outside the Aon complex was empty.

He put his phone to the centre of his forehead, as if pressing it hard enough against the bone there would tell him what he had to do.

He wondered whether he could engage the skills of his father's old friends, but since the deaths of the two men on the train, and the fact that Miller was standing inside the building, he concluded he had lost control of the Basques. There was no way they would help him find Joska. The only things he had in his deck were his old tricks.

He dialled another number, praying do a God he had long stopped believing in that it would connect.

"John, what the fuck is going on? Talk to me," Ander was unable to hide the desperation in his voice as he paced around the front of the Aon complex. He was gesticulating wildly as he spoke.

"I know as much as you, Ander," said John. He was confused, but this this didn't mean much to him. Aside from the paycheck he'd already be getting for completing his end of the bargain, he had no skin in this game. "I thought your boy was a shoe in, what with Marco and all that."

"Don't tell me my business, John. Remember who you're talking to," Ander grunted, "We need to get to Mixton to stop this going through. We could try his agent too. He must be connected with someone inside the club; I will find out who. But we still need the player. I need to talk to him. Please get me his number."

"Leave it with me," John replied, glad he hadn't gotten too much on the wrong side of Ander. The extra-curricular paychecks were supporting his family. "I'll call the liaison manager at Burnley now then forward you the number."

"And ask around about him. See if anyone has any dirt. Any secrets, anything we can use to stop this. We haven't got much time."

38

Time slowed down for Joska. She tried to get her bearings, but she didn't know this side of the mountains. Didn't recognise any of the place names as the car sped onwards, Micah taking the bends as though he were Fernando Alonso.

He cut in and out of the bends, the car repeatedly drifting into the opposite lane. Joska felt lucky that the roads were empty, but at the same time, it meant there was no one around to help her.

Rain had started to fall, drumming a pattern onto the windshield. Joska could barely see five metres in front of the car, but this didn't seem to bother Micah.

"Can't you just slow down," she tried to appeal to his reasonable side, "You have me in the car, I'm not going anywhere…" she pulled at the door handle to illustrate her point. It had locked automatically when the car had pulled away.

She saw Micah consider it for a second, but clearly nothing she was saying was getting through as the car careened around the next corner.

He hadn't told her where he was taking her, but she could only imagine they were on their way back to where she'd been held before. She didn't imagine her escape would be treated lightly.

"Why are you doing this?" she tried to get his attention again. "I saw you outside the hotel. Do you work for them? Whoever took me? So, you just do their bidding? Hurt girls? So, you're just a little bitch, does what he's told?" That worked. Micah took his foot off of the accelerator and scowled at her.

"I wonder if you'll be so cocky tomorrow, when your father fails in his business. You'll be assigned to me. I can tell you, I won't be as soft on you as the man who let you escape." Joska was shocked by the way he spoke to her. He had lost all of the charm he had shown her in the café.

"Please," she changed tack, shifted in her seat slightly so she could look directly at him. "Please don't make me go back there."

Joska reached out her hand and placed it on Micah's thigh, circling her fingers across the material of his trousers. Micah batted her hand away, and raised the back of his hand to her, stopping at the last second as she flinched back.

Micah scoffed. "You women are filthy, you think you can use your bodies to get what you want. Let me tell you, girl, I will show you what a bitch really is." He spat the words and Joska began to wonder if she had done the right thing.

She didn't know what was in store for her back in the hotel, but she knew it would be a lot worse than simply being held in a cell like before. She couldn't go back to that. She wouldn't. It was a fate worse than death.

Joska sat back in her seat and closed her eyes. She took several deep breaths, in and out, before opening them again. A solitary tear rolled down her cheek, tracing through the grime that caked her skin from the forest. She swiped it away, not wanting him to see her cry.

Satisfied he had put her in her place, Micah shifted up a gear again, pressing his foot into the floor and the car picked up speed again as they wound into another corner.

The rain continued to fall. Joska breathed in deeply, the petrichor scent hitting her nose, satisfying something deep and primal inside her. She looked out across the sierra, the rain blurring the mountains into the sky.

As Micah sped around another outside bend, Joska leaned over and grabbed the wheel and turned hard, sending the SUV clear onto the other side of the road. Micah barely had time to react before the car careened through the crash barrier, no match for the bulk of the SUV. Tyres screeched on the rain-soaked tarmac as he frantically slammed on the brakes. But it was too late. He turned to look at Joska as they flew off the side of the road, his eyes wide with fear.

It seemed like forever until the bottom of the car reconnected with the earth, and the impact flipped the SUV over onto its roof. There was a brief feeling of weightlessness as the car rolled over and Joska watched in horror as Micah's body fell headfirst into the roof which was now below them. She heard a sickening crunch as his head connected with the rocky floor below, and as the car continued to roll down the mountain, Micah's body ragdolled around, the weight of his figure bursting the airbag that had deployed in a meagre attempt to save his life.

After what seemed like minutes, but could only have been seconds, the car flipped once more onto its roof and continued to slide for several meters before coming to a stop.

Joska kept her eyes on Micah's lifeless body as she felt desperately for her seatbelt clip. She placed her hand on the clip and braced herself as she pressed the release button and fell head first into the ground. No time to raise her hands to brace the fall.

The smell of diesel seeped through the car.

Joska saw a small flame flickering in the corner of her eye.

Her vision blurred, like a vignette filter had been put over her eyes.

And then everything went black.

39

David sat inside the lobby, fixated on the news screen that showed a segment on the men who had followed him in the hotel. For a moment, he forgot where he was, forgot the task at hand.

His phone rang. Patrick.

"David," Patrick sounded worried, "Are you looking at the news?"

"Patrick," David tried to sound positive, "Don't worry about all of that. It's par for the course on deadline day – if it bleeds, it leads. How did it go this morning?"

"It was weird," said Patrick, "The doctor asked very invasive questions, it was like he was trying to trip me up. And I know he kept trying to cause me pain, grabbing my knee in weird places. It was like he wanted me to fail."

"He was probably just making sure he did a thorough job," David reassured Patrick, though he knew this was Ander's doing. No doubt he'd paid off the doctors to try to get Patrick to sink himself, and then if he didn't, to falsify his report. Paid off, or perhaps he was blackmailing them. It seemed more his style.

"Well, if you're sure, David," Patrick said, his unwavering trust in his agent showing itself again. David felt glad of the groundwork he'd put into their relationship.

"Patrick," he said, trying to shore up his client's worries, "I'm just at the Aon complex about to meet Aitor. I'll give you a call back later when everything's done and dusted. Put the champagne on ice."

The two made their goodbyes and David hung up the call.

His phone buzzed with a message from Annabel. She'd clearly been busy since he'd left her with Julia.

Not looking good for Patrick's medical. Definitely something dodgy with Ander and doctor. Someone pulling strings. Have guy at hospital trying to find out more.

David's heart sank a little. If Annabel was aware of bad news David had little doubt it was the truth.

He sent a reply:

Don't worry. Anaia's underestimated me. His problem. I can still do this. I need you to find anything re: relationship between Armstrong and knee specialist in hospital. Fishy.

Annabel confirmed she would follow up on the lead. She found David's defiance contagious.

"Any news John?" pleaded Ander as he powered back into the building.

"I got the number of the boy. That was easy. Married, three kids in case you need to find a way to use that. You'll enjoy this though," John said enthusiastically, "I called a guy

I know. He's got the biggest "poison drawer" I know of. Dirt on anyone and everyone. Was a key person in the phone hacking thing."

"Sounds like a good person to keep happy," said Ander.

"Don't worry, I've got enough on him to keep him onside for a long time. Good respectable family man, he is – except for his penchant for BDSM chemsex parties. Tells the wife he's off on golfing weekends." John laughed, but Ander was in no mood. He needed answers, now.

John noted the silence and carried on. "Anyway, journalism's come a long way since then. Well, at least the tech has – the ethics are still the same. We're now in the world of Pegasus," he paused for dramatic effect, "It's a spyware that can be installed on your phone without you even knowing. It can hack directly into your phone and extract all the information stored on there. Contacts, pictures, messages, the works. Shall I get my guy involved and we can get everything we need from Danny's phone and offer him some persuasion to not join United?"

"Yes, perfect," said Ander, starting to see chinks of light appear again. With Maier having failed the medical, he only needed to get Mixton out of the way and United would have no choice but to offer the contract to Markel. He would have done The Table's bidding. Joska would be safe.

"Thought you'd say that," said John, "Which is why I already had him start gathering all the dirt."

Ander laughed, starting to relax. This would soon all be over.

"Perfect! Send me over whatever you've got," Ander said gleefully.

David was still looking at the screens when Ander walked in, head held high, a different man to the one who'd scrambled out of sight just a short while ago. Something must have happened.

"Good day to be following the football news!" said Ander, taking a seat next to David, "So much drama! What's going to happen next, do you reckon?"

David ignored him and sipped his coffee. Something didn't feel right. He braced himself for what he knew was coming. He sat in silence, whilst Ander tapped away at his mobile phone.

"Ah," boomed Ander as he clasped his hands together, "Here we go!" David looked back to the screen.

BREAKING: Maier fails medical. United expected to sign another left-winger before close of transfer window.

David had knew it was coming, but it didn't change how sickening it felt.

"This happens when you don't listen to an agent as powerful as me," Ander smirked, "Did you really think you would get the deal over me, boy? I warned you to back off on several occasions."

David fought back the urge to launch himself at Ander, to plant a fist in his smug face.

Ander was relentless, "Good luck with your player. He will probably look for an agent who can finish a deal. All you give him is false hope!"

"You may have won the battle, Ander, but you will lose the war," said David, standing up and heading towards the main lobby. He needed some air. As he made his way across the entrance hall, he heard a voice call out.

"David! My boy, I'm so sorry to keep you waiting for so long. Would you mind coming to my office? I'd like to discuss the medical reports with you."

David tried desperately to figure out whether Aitor's tone was positive or negative.

"Hi Aitor," replied David as he tried to compose himself, "Sorry, I was just on the way to get some fresh air outside. I've just had to spend some time sitting with Ander Anaia," he paused, looking for a twinge of acknowledgement in Aitor's face. Aitor smiled conspiratorially and David breathed a sigh of relief. "I'll be with you in two minutes."

There was no sign of Victoria or Ander in the lobby as David made his way back in from outside. The crisp Manchester air had worked to revive him. He was a little surprised at the calm throughout the vast Aon complex. He had presumed he would find people running around all over the shop trying to push things over the line. Instead, it was ghostly silent.

On the short climb to Aitor's office he realised he hadn't even thought about how Patrick must be feeling. He needed to look after his player's feelings too. He was being selfish.

Patrick picked up immediately.

"They've dropped me back at the hotel instead of the training ground. Is everything ok, David?" asked Patrick.

He seemed anxious. David realised that they must have taken his phone from him during the medical, so he hadn't seen any of the news. There was no point in hiding it. He would check his phone soon enough. It was David's responsibility to keep Patrick informed.

"Just relax in the hotel. I'll update you as soon as I can. I'm about to meet with Aitor and sort this all out," David said, hoping that Patrick wouldn't see past his false confidence, "Just ignore the news when you check your phone. I knew that this might happen, but I'll do everything I can to put things right."

He knocked twice on Aitor's office door and held his breath.

"It's open," called a voice from inside.

David lingered outside for a moment longer before he walked in, affecting as much confidence as he could. He was dog tired and the news about Patrick had been a hammer blow. Part of him just wanted the day to end, wanted to move past it all. Wanted to get back to Annabel.

He was surprised to see Marco Anaia and the CEO, Andoni Andoni sat with Aitor around the low coffee table in the corner of the room. His nerves fluttered.

"Come in David, have a seat. Can I offer you a drink?" Aitor motioned towards the impressively stocked bar at the side of the office.

"No thanks, Aitor. It's far too early for me to have a drink," said David, smiling. It was first thing in the morning, but he noted that both Aitor and Marco nursed glasses of what looked like scotch. Clearly, they've seen one too many episodes of Mad Men, he thought. But the fact that they were drinking signalled to David that he could relax a little. This might not be as horrible a conversation as he'd anticipated.

He shook hands with Marco and Andoni. It was the first time that David had met the two legends of United and Bilbao and he found it difficult to hide his delight. Beneath it all, he was still just a boy who loved football. To that boy, this was a dream come true.

"Pleasure to meet you, David," said Andoni, the corners of his eyes crinkling as he smiled.

"The pleasure is all mine," replied David.

Marco sat in silence, rolling his glass between his hands. David felt like he was being examined.

"You've already seen the news about your boy's medical situation?" Aitor leaned over the desk towards David.

"Yes," choked David, looking at the ground to try and mask the disappointment across his face, "I've just seen it downstairs on the screen."

"Look, David. We like Patrick a lot. He was our first choice," explained Aitor, recapturing David's attention, "But the medical situation is a big problem. Our own medical team warned us that there might be an issue. We sent the reports to a knee expert in the hospital, and they agreed to give a second opinion. As we feared, this just confirmed the first one."

David could feel his cheeks flush. He felt like he'd been kicked in the stomach. He knew exactly what was coming next.

"Unfortunately, this means we can't move forward with this transfer. We all wanted to talk with you properly to explain the situation," finished Aitor.

David didn't know what to say or how to react. He just sat back in his seat, staring at his twiddling thumbs, and waiting for someone else to break the tense silence.

"I really liked Patrick as a player," said Marco, sounding genuinely hurt. David didn't understand. They all seemed gutted not to be able to sign Patrick – so why couldn't they? "I've been impressed by many of his games and our scouting department rated him as our number one target to sign in this window. This injury business is so disappointing. The whole club wishes him all the best back in Germany.".

Andoni grunted in agreement, "Please wish your boy all the best from our side. We hoped we could have signed him today, but these things happen in football unfortunately. We will explain it all honestly and professionally to the press later today."

David just listened. His heart ached. Not for the missed opportunity of glory, but for his family. What would his dad do now? They were already missing payments on utility bills. How long before the gas company cut off the supply. He couldn't let this stand. This was Ander's doing, and he had to undo it.

Suddenly there was a knock on the door, and the door swung open without giving anyone a chance to answer. David swivelled in his chair to find a small man in a suit who didn't look up from his phone as he spoke. A bead of sweat ran over the crease in his forehead. He'd clearly run up the stairs in a hurry. He ignored everyone else in the room and spoke directly to Aitor.

"Mr. Gaizka, sorry to disturb the meeting but we have an urgent problem." He wiped the sleeve of his jacket across his forehead, but the sweat was quickly replaced by more. Clearly working at a football training ground didn't require that you partake of the facilities.

He nodded towards the door, beckoning Aitor to follow him.

The men exchanged confused glances across the room. David suddenly felt as though this deadline day saga wasn't quite over yet.

Aitor Gaizka swiftly left the room, closely followed by the sweating man. Marco and Andoni got up to follow him without a word between them.

"Wait here David, we'll be back soon," said Andoni, turning back to him at the door.

David was now sat by himself in Aitor Gaizka's office. He had never felt more out of place in his life.

David felt like he could finally stop holding his breath and blew out in an exaggerated fashion, slumping back into his chair.

Whilst he had been listening to the others give their meaningless condolences and platitudes, he had felt his phone constantly buzzing in his pocket. He took it out and saw a seemingly endless line of messages. As he anticipated, everyone was writing to him about the injury blow. He would deal with those later. He had to call Annabel.

"Are you not reading your messages?" Annabel cried.

"I'm sorry, I wasn't alone," replied David apologetically, "I'm still in Aitor's room but sat on my own now. I'm waiting for them to get back. We were chatting about the injury, but someone interrupted because there's some problem. I'm not sure what's going on."

"It's all over the news. They're trying to sign this boy from Burnley instead. He is having his medical as we speak. The media have literally surrounded the hospital. It's the story of the day," said Annabel.

It was not what David wanted to hear.

"Did you get anything regarding the relationship between Ander and the medical team?" he asked hopefully.

"Funny you should ask. Not ten minutes ago a package arrived at my desk with no sender details."

David felt a flicker of hope, "And?" He demanded to know more. "What was in it? Chocolates?" He was in no mood.

"Cool your boots, Davey. No, not chocolates, though thanks for offering," Annabel skirted over his rudeness, forgiving him, it had been a long day already and it wasn't even lunchtime yet. "It's a USB stick with a single audio clip on it. You can hear a conversation between none other than Rob Armstrong, and someone at the hospital. It has to be this other doctor, with the 'second opinion'" said Annabel.

David's face beamed with a smile, "Let me guess; it's Armstrong telling the knee specialist to confirm his reports?"

"Ten points, Davey!" Annabel said and David clenched one fist in victory.

"I knew it. When Ander called me months ago and asked me to back off from this deal, I knew he wasn't going to make it easy. But I thought I was just fighting against nepotism. The Basque Mafia. The Anaia brothers," chuckled David, "I knew he was dodgy, who doesn't, but I never thought he'd take it this far. But we've got him now – even if they can't link it back to Ander, the whole thing about Patrick's knee falls apart."

"I'm on my way to you now. Hold tight," Annabel said, and David's heart swelled.

The game was still on.

40

Danny Mixton, the Burnley winger, left the private hospital through a discrete entrance at the back of the building. None of the media that formed the crowd at the front realised that he had left.

His medical was only just due to begin and usually, players would leave through the main entrance so that the media could snap photos and ask for comments from the club's latest signing. But not this time.

His agent hurried frantically behind him.

"What's going on? Are you mad?" he exclaimed desperately, "How can you just leave the medical like that?"

Danny stopped in his tracks as he turned to face his agent.

"No, I'm not mad. I just don't want this deal to happen," he said stubbornly, "It doesn't feel right. I feel like I'm a last-minute choice. They would never have signed me if the lad from Germany passed his medical today, would they?"

His agent had a face like thunder. He couldn't believe what he was hearing.

"Are you joking?" he yelled, "This is Manchester United we are talking about! Two hours ago, you couldn't wait to join them! You told me it was your childhood dream and how thankful you are that you're finally getting this opportunity. Your salary was about to triple! What on Earth could have changed your mind suddenly?"

Danny ignored his agent's desperate search for answers as he got into the blacked-out car waiting for them. He'd made his decision. Or, rather, it had been made for him.

He liked his agent and didn't want to keep things from him. He wished he could tell him what had happened back in the doctor's room, but that conversation could never be spoken of to anybody apart from the two that were present.

When Danny first met Armstrong for his medical, he had been brimming with excitement. It was short lived. He never expected anything like what had happened next. It replayed over in his head as the car pulled away.

Armstrong had introduced himself with an exaggerated sense of authority, "You must be excited" Armstrong had said, "But before we start, I've been asked to forward you this."

He had handed Danny a sports bag.

"I'll leave the room," Armstrong had said, "Call me in once you've finished and we'll start the examination."

"Will do," Danny had replied.

He opened the bag slowly. There were a few packages inside. A letter sat on top bearing a hastily scrawled message.

Leave without doing the medical and go back to Burnley. You will be given £2.5million in cash, and we will not release the photos contained in the plastic bag. We also have videos! Choose sensibly.

Danny's stomach had dropped. Was this some kind of joke?

He opened the first plastic bag and found bundles of notes. It was surprising how little space two and a half million pounds took up, he thought.

Something told him that the other bag would be more troublesome. As he ripped it open, a handful of photos fell to the floor. They were images from a big party in one of his Burnley teammate's summer houses last year. The photos showed the faces of plenty of naked women and more than five of his teammates. Four of them, including Danny, had wives and kids. Worse still, in some of them his teammates could be seen taking cocaine.

The impact of these photos had the desired effect. Danny had sunk into the seat behind him, staring at the photos in his lap.

If they came out in the press, it would destroy his life. His career, his family, and that of his teammates.

He hid the letter and the photos in the inner pocket of his jacket. The box lay open on the examination bed.

He called out to Armstrong.

"I've changed my mind," he began, unable to bring himself to look the doctor in the eyes, "I'm not going through with this today."

"What?" Armstrong gasped dramatically, "What's going on Danny?"

Danny hadn't answered. His face was stricken with guilt and his mind was doing somersaults.

"Everyone is waiting for this transfer. Let me talk with your agent," Armstrong pleaded, Danny not picking up on the levels of overacting "Let me call the clubs first. I'm sure we all can convince you to stay and sign. The opportunity to sign with a club like this might not come again."

"I just don't feel it's the right decision," sighed Danny finally, "It just hit me out of nowhere. I'm happy at Burnley and I want to stay there. That's it."

"What was the…"

"Just fan mail," lied Danny, "A fan who wanted to have the first signature. It's a replica kit."

He had left as quickly as he could, bundling his things into the bag and pushing out of the door without looking back.

Armstrong let out a hint of a smirk as he watched him leave.

He picked up the phone that hung on the wall.

"It's done," he said, and disconnected, thinking about what he would spend the money on first.

41

The silence inside Aitor's office was interrupted by a raised voice reverberating through the door of the office.

"Who's that, creating a scene?" pondered Andoni.

"I'll give you three guesses," Marco said, sighing1He always felt a wave of shame and guilt, as if he was to blame for the way his brother was.

Andoni added his sigh to the room as Ander burst in, a Cheshire Cat grin spread across his face.

"Gentlemen," he said, patting his brother on the shoulder, "It's nice to finally meet you all in the same room. Including you, David!"

There was a brief pause as Ander moved the last chair in the room in front of the desk as he glared at Aitor. The arrogance he exuded was almost admirable. It was certainly tone deaf.

"What do you want, Ander?" muttered Aitor.

"What do I want?" he scoffed, "I'm cleaning up your fucking mess! I should be asking what you wanted with your ludicrous targets? The first one has a broken knee and the second one walks out of a medical to go back home to his mummy. What kind of recruitment is that?"

He leaned forward, forcing his point as Aitor broke his stare.

"Where did you learn this method of recruitment? Oh sorry, this is your first job in football. How can I forget? Well, you certainly act like it is" he let out a mean-spirited cackle. "Anyway, at least I'm actually here to sort your mess. I've just sent Markel to do his medical. In a couple of hours, he'll come straight here for the signing session. Bilbao have already agreed on the terms. They'll get five-million as a transfer fee and another five in transfer bonuses. Personally, I will not see any of that. They promised twenty percent, but I'll be sending all of that to social projects and charities in the Basque region. Even my fee from you guys will go to projects in Bilbao, to the people in the prisons and their families who are victims of the oppression of the regime in Madrid. I will give you a list with prisons and families that I want the money to go to."

Ignoring David, he looked to his brother and felt a wave of shame flush over him as he remembered the barrel, he'd bent him over. One day soon he would have a chance to explain everything. Would have a chance to ask for forgiveness. He locked eyes with each man across the table.

"It's time that you all fucking wake up. When was the last time you guys have been home? You have all forgotten your roots and history. We are Basque people and Basque people always help each other. Especially when they are family and friends," finished Ander, "You lot should be ashamed of yourselves."

No one knew what to say. Silence descended upon the office once again. Aitor was gripping the arms of his chair so hard that his knuckles were as white as the leather upholstery.

David looked around awkwardly, feeling as though he was caught in a crossfire that he didn't really understand.

"I've already given the exclusive on the news to Sky Sports," Ander continued.

Andoni scowled at Ander.

"Enough! Ander, without your brother you would be nothing," he shouted, "Nothing! You're a scumbag. Everyone knows it. Your throw your weight about, and god knows what else you're involved in. If being Basque means being like you, then I'd rather not return."

Everyone in the room looked shocked. No one had ever heard Andoni raise his voice before.

Marco had had enough now. "Everyone stop, now!" he yelled, splaying his hands in the air, "I can't listen to this anymore. We are family and friends, and we have to make the best out of this situation. What's the point in fighting each other? Leave it for another time. Put our differences aside and let's finish this window by signing the boy. We can discuss our thoughts and feelings afterwards, whatever they might be!"

He shook his head in disappointment at Ander. A flash of guilt flicked across his brother's face.

Everyone in the room knew they had to do this deal now. Marco was right. There was no other choice.

In the melee, David had snuck out of the ground after seeing a text from Annabel. She was too afraid to come nearer to the ground, cautious that Ander might have employed people to keep an eye out for her. He found her sat in the car that Malik had let them borrow a few streets away. He tapped on the window, and she looked up with a broad smile.

"Ready?" asked David, wearing a steely, defiant air. "Let's do this. Let's sink Anaia completely."

Annabel grin spread even wider. She pulled a small package from her pocket. "The USB stick. You won't believe what's on it."

David felt a thump of elation rush through him, "Who sent it to you? What was said about Patrick?"

"No idea. It was just left on my desk. Whoever it was clearly didn't want Anaia to make his deal. Part of me wonders if it's someone at The Table – they're renowned gamblers. Most agents are, right? Wouldn't put it past them to be doing some matched betting on Ander's boy getting in at United."

"Well, whoever it was, they're a guardian angel," said David. I'll see you later, I need to get this in front of the United board right now."

"Go, go!" she made an exaggerated shooing motion. He grabbed one of her hands and looked deep into her eyes. "Thank you, Annabel. I don't know wha—"

"Go!" she said, "Stop dawdling!"

On the way back to Aitor's office, he called Patrick again.

"What's going on, David?" Patrick asked, not even trying to hide his anxiety. David couldn't blame him, Patrick had been alone all day, with only the news to keep him company. It was enough to send anyone crazy, even if they weren't directly involved in the outcome.

David could sense the hurt in his voice and was so relieved that he was able to reassure him. The envelope in his hand had changed the whole situation.

"Don't worry Patrick. That's just nonsense football reporting." It was a half-truth. "Everything is going ahead. It's not been quite as smooth as we could have all hoped, but I'll try to explain all that later." He promised himself he would. He had worked hard to gain Patrick's trust, he needed to keep it.

"Let me deal with this stuff, I just need you to take a cab in half an hour and come to the training ground. I will get the signing sorted," said David comfortingly.

"Okay, David," Patrick was still hesitant, "I don't know what you are doing… but I trust you. Don't let me down."

"Thanks Patrick, that's all I need you to do. See you later."

He made his way through security again, flashing his visitor badge and the woman who had let him through earlier gave a curt nod as she ushered him back through.

"Just go straight through, sir," she said, "No need to give you the full cavity search." It was against policy, but David had the sneaking suspicion that this woman had had more than one run in from the older Anaia and was helping David in his mission to take Ander out of the picture.

He could hear the raised voices of the men inside Aitor's office from the bottom of the staircase. He entered the room without hesitating this time, but it seemed as though the argument was dying down now. Seemed as though someone had won.

"This is our last option, there is no debate," admitted Andoni reluctantly, "We will sign your player, Ander."

Despite his arrogance, Ander was momentarily speechless. After everything that had happened, this still felt like the victory he'd been after.

"You may have won today but this will have consequences for sure," added Andoni.

Ander laughed, "You said the same thing last summer, and look where we are now! Even my brother didn't want to help me this time. I did it all by myself and here we are, I've still succeeded." He beat his hand against his chest as he spoke, punctuating every point.

"I beg to differ," interjected David. Four heads shot round to see him standing in the doorway. It seemed they hadn't notice him enter.

"What do you mean little boy? Say it with your chest, or just shut up and listen," Ander said.

There was silence in the room.

"I've learned many things in the last few days, thanks to you guys," said David, "I've seen how an agent like Ander could fool you all to the point of signing his player." He turned to Ander, "But you made one mistake. A big one."

The three United men were looking at Ander now, trying to gauge his reaction. Ander screwed his hands into fists.

"Until now, I just watched and listened. Now it's time for me to talk and you to listen," he said confidently, taking a deep breath. He turned to Aitor, "Patrick is one-hundred-percent fit. I know this because I paid for two independent medical examinations in Munich. The first was with Muller Wohlfart, who's looked after Bayern and the German national team for more than twenty-five years. The second time I sent him to one of the best knee specialists in the world, Dr Ramon Cugat. Both of them confirmed what we already knew. Patrick is fit as a fiddle. In fact, Cugat's report said that his operated knee is even stronger than his other one," laughed David.

"Those are just other opinions David," Aitor interrupted him, "We're the ones signing the players so we will do our own examination. We don't need the opinion of other doctors." His hackles were up since his run in with Ander.

"But he was doomed to fail," David began lining up his coup de grace, "You guys need to root around your staff – there are too many people here on the take. What I have here is proof that both doctors you employed to do Patrick's medical are on Ander's payroll," He patted his breast pocket, shifting his gaze from Aitor to Ander who was completely crestfallen.

Aitor fell back in his chair, shock plastered across his face but also the subtle hint of a smile in the corner of his mouth.

Andoni and Marco looked at one another, not quite believing what they were hearing.

"What are you trying to say, David?" said Andoni after what seemed like an eternity.

"Choose your next words carefully," Marco added. David couldn't figure out if it was a threat.

"He paid your medical team," David pointed to Ander, "Armstrong might work for you guys, but he serves Ander. He lied in the report."

"Bullshit!" yelled Ander, moving towards David and raising a fist. The other three men stood up to intervene. Ander unclenched his fist and jabbed a finger into David's chest. "You can't prove that, you son of a bitch. Unbelievable. What a bad loser."

"Ander! Sit back down!" yelled Marco, "Don't embarrass yourself."

"But we got a second opinion from someone in the hospital. A knee specialist," said Andoni, confused.

"What you got was two piles of bullshit. The doctor who gave a second opinion is a friend of Armstrong. He takes a cut. They're all in the same boat, captained by Ander." David felt it best to keep the information about The Table under wraps now. To most it was a conspiracy theory. He didn't want to ruin his credibility.

"Stop saying things you can't prove," said Ander, his face was a crimson red, fuelled by anger. Fuelled by fear.

"These are the two independent medical reports for Patrick," said David, remaining calm and ignoring Ander as he passed over the documents, "For your records," he added.

Andoni lay them on the desk in front of him and began to scan over them.

"More importantly," David said, raising his voice to recapture Andoni's attention, "Here is a USB stick with a recording of the conversation between Armstrong and his friend from the hospital."

He pulled the device from his jacket pocket, held it in the air trapped between his fingers as everyone in the room stared at it. Even Ander fell silent.

"I will either give it to you Andoni, to the ownership or maybe directly to the police. I haven't decided which yet. I've listened to the audio. In the conversation it can be heard that there was a second payment left on Armstrong's desk. That one must be from someone in this club," said David. He looked at each of the men, trying to see if any had reacted to his accusation.

"How did you get this?" asked Andoni startled.

"I got it from a journalist investigating Ander and Aitor's relationship with the club," smirked David.

"What do you want then?"

"Justice," said David without hesitation. "Nothing more, nothing less. You will sign Patrick today. He is on his way over here as we speak. If everything goes well, then you can have this, and you can start cleaning out this corrupt house that you run before the owners arrive. I hear on the news that they've chartered a jet over here."

As David delivered his monologue, they heard the door slam. Ander was nowhere to be seen.

42

Ander burst through the main entrance of the Aon training complex, barging through the security staff and into the car park.

He pawed at his phone, unable to focus in his panic. Eventually he made the right combination of taps and raised the phone to his ear. He carried on walking as the phone rang. Through the line of trees that protected the players at the training ground from prying eyes. Past the sentry boxes and raised barriers and across the road into a scrubby patch of gravel opposite that opened up into acres of barren agricultural land.

"Come on, come on, pick up the fucking phone," he said out loud.

The line connected and once again the other caller elided any conversational formalities.

"I thought I told you we were done, Anaia," the voice matched the gravel scraping beneath the leather soles of Ander's shoes. "I've got two funerals to arrange and a lot of bail money to pay. I'll make sure to add the costs to your invoice."

“Please,” Ander was desperate, “I need your help just one last time. They have my daughter. If you won’t do it for me, do it for my fathe—”

“You dare invoke your father’s memory to me? He would be sick at the way you conduct yourself. Your father was a man of honour, a proud Basque. You are a disgrace to our country.” Ander’s head sunk low as he heard these words. He had let greed get in the way of everything. And now… Joska.

He tried to respond but heard the click of the line going dead and the long monotone of the dropped line.

He turned to face the wasteland opposite him. Electricity pylons jutted out of the grey earth into the melancholy north-western sky. He pulled back his hand and threw his phone as hard as he could, releasing a primeval scream.

It was over.

***

Hours later, Ander sat with Markel in the hotel lobby, trying to explain the situation. He felt his career as an agent crumbling around him.

“You lied to me, Ander. Something you promised never to do,” Markel rested a hand on the telescopic handle of his suitcase. He was dressed ready for a flight: matching tracksuit, sunglasses perched on top of his head. He was going home.

“Worse than that, you embarrassed me.”

"Our own blood did all of this to you!" Ander pleaded, "I have been let down as much as you have. Your transfer was blocked by Aitor, Marco, Andoni!"

Markel sat expressionless as Ander continued.

"I am so sorry, but I never planned for betrayal. I thought the men we were dealing with were true Basques," Ander would say anything to keep his client. He had lost everything else. "What didn't happen today will happen in January. I promise you," he added desperately.

"I'm tired of your promises, Ander. I'm not sure what you want me to say. How can I go back to Bilbao now? My family, my friends and my teammates. Everyone will laugh at me, I've let them all down because I trusted you. I don't think we should work together anymore," said Markel bluntly, "I will go on my own from now on. Not with you. Not with someone who doesn't keep their word."

Markel stood up and walked away before Ander had a chance to respond. Ander's head sank into his hands.

As Markel walked off out of the hotel, the man sat along from Ander began to laugh. Ander turned, his face and recognised the man immediately. It was Jack Farmington, the Director of The Table. Markel stood up and walked away before Ander had a chance to respond. Ander stared after him for a while before his head sank into his hands.

He heard a "tut tut" over to his right, cutting through the hospital ward silence of the hotel lobby. Ander raised his head and turned to the disturbance. A man, dressed elegantly in a Tom Ford suit stood in the middle of the tiled floor staring directly at him. His eyes wore an exaggerated frown and he jutted out his bottom lip, tipping his head to one side.

"Poor old Ander," Jack Farmington broke the spell, straightening up, picking a speck of dust from the shoulder of his jacket.

"Hola my friend," he said, still laughing, in a perfect imitation of Ander, "What's happened here then? You promised The Table this deal would happen, and you couldn't deliver. You know what that means Ander!"

As he delivered the line, the automatic door glided open as two men walked through. They wore serious expressions as they came to join Farmington, standing either side of him.

Ander shrank back into his seat.

"Please, my daughter – she's done nothing. She doesn't deserve this..."

"You should've thought of that, my son," Farmington said, a malicious smile unfurling across his face, "And anyway, it's not quite so clear cut as that anymore," he adjusted his tie, cleared his throat.

Ander shot him a glance, "What do you mean? What have you done? You animals. You fuckin—" He felt as though he were tensing every muscle in his body.

"Ah, that famous temper. Clouds the judgement, all that rage. Probably where she got it from," Farmington had a faraway look in his eye, as if accessing some packed away memory. "Well, you might like to hear that she gave us the right run-around, your little girl."

Ander's heart leapt with a strange sense of pride. His daughter, his Joska had given these thugs a bit of Basque grit.

"All for nothing in the end, though..." Farmington trailed off, "Shame. Pretty young thing. Well, enough of this – we must get going. Will you come willingly, or will the boys have to persuade you?" On cue, the two men standing astride Farmington stepped forward, each taking Ander under one arm.

"Get your hands off of me," Ander shook himself free and made a lunge for Farmington, grabbing onto one of his lapels.

"Now look, you monster – you tell me where my daughter is or so help me, I'll—"

Farmington cut Ander off with a swift backhanded slap.

"I'd be very careful about what you say next, Ander. It will determine how long this next bit takes. Personally, I can't see the point of drawing it out, but Jamie here..." he slapped a hand onto the shoulder of one of his henchmen. Ander noticed the opal set in gold that adorned Farmington's pinkie, the blackness drawing his eye deeper and deeper.

Farmington brought Ander back to reality with a bang.

"...He likes to take his time."

The man smiled and took Ander underneath the arm again and the two men began to usher Ander through the sliding doors, Farmington in close step behind them. Ander could hear the leather of his soles slap against the paving slabs outside.

The sun was too bright, after the relaxing artificial glow inside the lobby and Ander closed his eyes, letting the men guide him to wherever they were taking him.

"Please," Ander said, "Just tell me where Joska is. She is all I have left."

"Well," Farmington said, "This is awkward..."

He didn't need to finish. Ander let out a wail of despair and a wave of nausea washed over him. He turned his head to the unnamed goon and let out a spray of vomit. The man dropped Ander's arm and called out.

Quick as a flash, Ander wheeled on the other heavy and launched himself at him, flailing wildly with his arms and legs. Barely any of the blows connected in a significant way, but the confusion he had caused gave him enough time to turn on his heels and run as quickly as he could in the opposite direction.

43

Joska's eyes were still closed, but she had the peculiar feeling of falling.

She gathered herself and prised one eye open but was met by a bright white glare that forced it shut again.

She felt as though she were floating, like a gentle, firm hand was dragging her upwards. Towards what?

Deprived of sight, she listened out for clues as to her situation. Everything sounded muffled, like she was underwater.

But they'd been on top of a mountain. There was no water here.

Where had they been going?

Who was 'they'? Who had she been with?

She tried again to open her eyes and this time managed to bring a hand up to her face to block out the glare. A sharp pain shot through her side, and she cried out.

It took a few seconds for her eyes to focus. The vague shape of distant mountains hazed into view. She managed to turn her head to the left, the pain shooting through her again, and saw vast green-brown scrubland stretching off before losing itself in a line of fir trees.

She was alive, then.

She heard a voice now, though she couldn't make out what it was trying to tell her. It was as though someone were speaking into a pillow, the sound buffeted her ears as a series of marshmallow-soft syllables. She turned her head again towards the source of the noise.

"...not to... Need to as... see if any... broken..."

Joska's hand reached up to her shoulder where she felt the pulling and connected with a strong hand, rough. She tapped the hand as it kept on dragging her.

Micah.

Joska's eyes shot open wide, and she grabbed at the hand, clawing at it, throwing it off of her. She fought against the pain that flared all through her left side and twisted round and away from his grasp.

As she reached standing, Joska felt her knees buckle beneath her and she stumbled forwards, managing to stay upright by grasping the clothing of the man in front of her.

Micah. She remembered. He had been taking her somewhere. Somewhere bad. Somewhere she didn't want to go. She pushed at him again.

A voice rang out clearer now.

"Hey, woah lady, chill."

She felt hands clamp down on her shoulders now, steadying her. Helping her to stand.

"Micah that guy in the truck? You don't need to worry about him no more, trust me."

What was he saying? It took Joska all of her energy to focus. As she regained her composure, she looked at the man who had been dragging her. Boy, really. Some kid, hair long, scruffy beard, wearing an oversized t-shirt, shorts, hiking boots. The sleeves on his shirt were rolled up so Joska could see the tan line. Or maybe it was dirt on his skin. Smoke. The skin on his forearms was swollen and red, blistered and cracked in places.

"Who are you?" she eventually managed to ask.

"Who am I? Who are *you* more like. All I know is one minute I'm finishing up my morning snack, about to hit the trail again. Then all of a sudden," he made a series of energetic sound effects, "Your car comes flying through the air above. It was totally wild!" He looked wide-eyed at Joska, but then averted his eyes.

"Sorry, I shouldn't get so carried away. Your friend – Micah? He didn't make it. By the time I got to the wreck, I had to make a choice. Way he looked, he'd snapped his neck – always wear a seatbelt, yo," His monologue darted all over the place, and he could barely contain the excitement in his voice, despite himself. "I could see you were breathing, so I got in there and hauled you out. Just in time, I guess." He gestured off into the distance and Joska followed where he was pointing.

The car that Micah had been driving was still ablaze. It sat on its roof, the windscreen shattered, airbags deployed and deflated. Joska couldn't quite believe that she'd been riding in the vehicle. That she'd made it out alive. It was a wreck.

"Listen, I called the police…" the boy hesitated, "I hope that's okay? Ambulance, too. I just thought it was the thing to do." Clearly, he sensed something strange in the way that Joska was acting. She looked at him, trying to make sense of what he was saying.

"He's dead? The man in the car?" Joska asked, her brain was still catching up with events, taking longer than usual to process what she was seeing and hearing.

The boy didn't say anything, just looked at the floor.

"I never saw a dead body before, but there was no way that guy survived that fall. And for sure he's not alive now."

Joska jumped at the boy, throwing both arms around him. She let out a scream of pure unadulterated joy. Pulling up as the pain shot through her side again, she held the boy at arm's length. His face was a picture. As if the situation couldn't get much weirder than it already was, here was a girl cheering the death of the man she'd been riding with.

"What did you say your name was?" Joska asked.

"… Lucas," said the boy, still aghast.

"Lucas, do you still have you phone?"

"Sure, here," he said, and dug into one of the many pockets in his outfit. He fished out an ancient 'dumbphone' and handed it to Joska. She dialled the number and pressed the call button.

It took several attempts, but eventually the call was answered.

"What? What the hell do you want? Who the hell are you?" the voice sounded exhausted, cracked and parched as if they'd been crying.

"Daddy," Joska said, smiling, "It's me. I'm safe." Tears began to roll down her face as Joska fell to the floor.

Ziggy reached out to break her fall and sat with her. He places a consoling arm around her shoulder and the two sat there, watching the horizon, listening for the sound of sirens.

44

David was sitting in the first-class carriage, waiting for the train back home to London to depart the station. As always, he was reading the latest sports news on his phone. This time, it was slightly different. All of the news was about his deal. Social media was aflame with positivity about Patrick's signing.

As he skimmed through, a video call came through. It was William.

David swiped to answer and was met by an image of William, aviator shades wrapped around his head, walking through a sun-drenched London street.

"We've already bought the cigars and I'm on my way to buy some proper whisky. Jose's been into our friends at 39 Steps to get the roof top spot. When are you back?" William asked, beaming.

"So, Jose's out of hospital?" David felt a sense of deep relief wash through him. He felt guilty that he hadn't been able to check in on his friends since Ander's heavies had assaulted Jose.

"*Si, amigo* – I am here, all in one piece," William swung the camera to Jose whose shades barely covered the puffiness and bruising around his face. He had a deep laceration under one eye, held together with stitches. "Well, almost one piece…" he gave a full-mouthed grin, showing his teeth. One of his front incisors was snapped in half. "I might get a gold one put in," Jose laughed.

"Well, if nothing else, you'll have a cool scar…"

"Didn't fancy saying goodbye?" a female voice behind him interrupted.

"Annabel?" said David turning around excitedly. He could hear William and Jose scrabbling around on the phone, trying to catch a glimpse of David's 'mystery girl'.

It was her.

She gave him a warm, affectionate smile, "I had to see you before you went back to London," said Annabel. "Did you really think you could just leave like that?"

"Boys. I've got to go. Get one more cigar, eh?" and to the protestations of his friends, he hung up the phone.

"I knew you were busy!" said David, turning back to Annabel, "I wasn't sure what to do when you said you couldn't meet me at the station after the signing."

"I wanted to surprise you! I've got the next couple of days off work. Thought I'd come and stay in London with you, if it's okay with you?" she said as she sat down next to him. "I've still not met William and Jose. But…" she pretended to pick up her bag again, sat up from her seat, "I can take the next stop and go back to Manchester if you're busy?" she added.

"No, no, no! That's the best idea I've heard all week!" grinned David, grabbing her arm and pulling her back down to the seat next to him.

Annabel reached for his hand. David felt pure joy. He had never experienced a feeling of contentment like it. He'd finished the deal, and now this.

45

"So," Annabel said, jolting David out of his daze, "How was the signing in the end. What happened to Ander?" she asked enthusiastically.

"After I explained to them that I had proof and told them what I wanted, they just sat there in silence. It was brilliant!" he chuckled, "Andoni announced that they were going to agree to sign Patrick and Ander just stormed out. I've not heard from him since. I spoke to one of the security guards at Aon. She said she saw him walk straight out of the Aon centre and across the road into the fields over there. Apparently, he was going completely crazy. I guess he lost his place at The Table…"

Annabel opened her mouth to respond, but something caught her eye out of the window.

"I don't believe it," she said, her eyes widening.

David turned to see what she had spotted and was greeted with the spectacle of Ander Anaia pacing across the platform heading directly for the First Class coach.

He heaved himself onto the carriage and barged into the carriage, immediately filling it with his presence.

"David. Ms. Frost," he nodded to both David and Annabel, "So, this is one of your famous English trains, yes? How quaint," Ander looked around disapprovingly at the vacuum formed plastic walls, the tiny Formica tables and the lurid purple polyester seats.

"What do you want, Ander? You lost. Don't make this harder on yourself than it already is." David was filled with confidence.

"David, come – where are your manners? I have little to say to you except 'well played', I suppose. Ms. Frost, it is you I am here to see." Ander turned to Annabel, who returned his look with a raised eyebrow. As far as she was concerned, she never wanted to see the man again. Ander was sweating from his run across the train station, years of cigar smoking meant his lungs were struggling to catch a breath.

"Ander, I'm in the same boat as David here. I've got nothing to say to you except to let you know that your time is marked. I was having trouble tying this whole story together, but now with what you've put us through with these ex-ETA guys, and the shit you pulled with Patrick's medical, I've got my lynchpin. You're running out of time, Ander..." Annabel could barely look at him.

"You think I don't know you've been building a story on me all this time? What if I told you I had something for you? Something that could really help you elevate your journalistic status." Ander paused, letting the comment settle. "What if I could give you The Table?"

Annabel and David looked at one another.

"Sit down, Ander," David said, "This had better be good."

Acknowledgements

There are several people who made this book possible, so I would like to thank Tom Witcomb for his editorial expertise and guidance through the publication process, Jaime Witcomb for her help getting the book into the hands of readers, and Jamie Khan for helping to kick everything off.

Printed in Great Britain
by Amazon